Most of Madison's life has been dedicated to finding the lost pride and their temple. The temple is rumored to heal people and even bring them back from death, and that's what Madison needs. He became a historian thanks to his grandmother, and he'll do whatever he can to being her back.

He just didn't think that would include getting shot at.

Ford is an outcast of his own making. He might have been part of the lost pride when he was a child, but he hasn't been in years, and he intends to keep things that way, even though his brother is the pride's alpha. He's fine being a guide to rich tourists who want to get their thrill exploring the jungle.

Except that Madison isn't a tourist, and he's looking for something specific and sacred to its guardians. He's not sure he can trust Ford, but Ford is the only person who's there for him when the bullets start flying. They don't have a choice and will have to trust each other if they want to find the temple.

And survive.

Romancing the Wolf
Copyright © 2023 Catherine Lievens
ISBN: 978-1-4874-3894-4
Cover art by Angela Waters

Published by eXtasy Books Inc

Look for us online at:
www.eXtasybooks.com

ROMANCING THE WOLF

BY

CATHERINE LIEVENS

CHAPTER ONE

"Is it true that you're a shifter?"

Madison almost groaned at the question. He'd known it was coming. Every year, at least one student wanted to know if he was a shifter. He'd tried everything to get around the question. He'd ignored it, had told the student it was none of their business, and had answered honestly. There was no right way to go about it, especially when his students were always curious.

He looked at the young people gathered in the classroom. It was normal for them to want to know if he was a shifter, since he taught shifter history. He had no doubt there were a few shifters in the class, and if he lied, they might wonder why he was doing so and have more questions.

He sighed and nodded curtly. "I am." That shouldn't be the reason these students wanted to take this course, but every year, a number of them just wanted to gawk at the shifter professor.

"What kind of shifter?" another student asked, this one a woman.

Madison needed this line of questioning to stop. "Everyone in my family is a wolf shifter," he answered before gesturing at the screen. "Now, if you're done asking personal questions, we can get back to the class."

There were a few whispers, but Madison ignored them. It had taken him a while to learn to do so, but eventually he'd managed, and now, at thirty-eight years old, he knew how to deal with students and that sometimes it was better to ignore

1

the ones whispering behind his back than confront them about not listening to him.

Not everyone was as passionate as he was about shifter history. It probably had to do with the fact that there weren't that many shifters around, plus that most tended to stick to their family and pack and avoid humans. They weren't in hiding, but they liked their peace, and things seldom were peaceful when humans were involved.

"Now, as most of you probably already know, the first written testimony about shifters come from missionaries," he explained. "There are stories of shifters living in Europe before then, but they hid. The shifters in the countries the missionaries were sent to were more open about what they were, though."

Madison had repeated the same info time and time again, but it never got old. He loved this subject, and while he didn't love teaching, doing so meant he had enough funds to poke around ruins and jungles when he wasn't teaching during the summer. It wasn't nearly enough to make him happy, but he didn't have a choice.

He'd worked in the jungle over the previous summer and was sure he'd been close to finding an ancient shifter temple. He'd had to come home before he did, but he'd go back. Besides, one of his friends had stayed back, and if they were lucky, she'd find the temple before next summer. Madison didn't care if he had to take a leave of absence. If anyone found that temple, he'd be there, exploring it.

Teaching drained him, just like spending time with people in general. He was ready for some alone time when he left the classroom, but of course he had to pause to talk to some of the students. Once that was done, he almost ran away, needing to hide in his office for a while.

Things never went the way he wished. Before he could step in through the door, his phone rang. He juggled his bag and computer to get the phone out of his pocket, thankful he'd remembered to turn down the volume. His mother knew not to call when he was teaching, but she had a habit of waiting only a few seconds after his class was supposed to be over to try. Several times, he'd had to interrupt the end of class to answer, and while today wasn't one of those days, he still scowled at his mother's name on the screen.

He didn't want to answer. She'd call again if he didn't, but it would give him a moment of respite, and that was what he needed. There was a family run coming up, and his mother would demand he be there, which was pretty much the last thing he wanted to do.

Unfortunately for him, there would be no way out of it.

But he didn't have to think about it now, so he pushed his phone back into his pocket and strode into his office. He dumped what he was holding onto his desk, then flopped into his chair and tilted his head back to stare at the ceiling.

He was exhausted. He wanted to return to the jungle but couldn't afford it. He couldn't afford to lose his job, either, which was what would happen if he said *fuck it* and left.

He sighed and decided to do the next best thing. He couldn't go to the jungle, but he could call Ashley. She was living his dream life in the jungle, and while Madison was jealous as hell, he wouldn't mind living vicariously through her.

He also wanted to make the phone call before his mother called back.

He got his phone out again, dialed Ashley's number, and waited. She didn't always answer, and it wasn't a surprise when Madison didn't even get a ring. Cell phone service was spotty at best in the jungle.

With a sigh, he put down his phone and turned on his computer. He smiled when he saw he had a new email from Ashley, especially when he saw the email included pictures. Had she found something? She would have called if she had, but if cell service wasn't good, she might not have been able to. Excitedly, he clicked on the email. He ignored the few lines of text and opened the pictures, tilting his head at the sight of a stone wall.

It looked old, and if he squinted, he could see what remained of ancient designs covering it. He couldn't tell what they depicted, but his heart beat faster. Most of the wall was covered by vegetation, a sure sign it was somewhere in the jungle and that it was well hidden.

He clicked through more pictures. The same wall appeared several times, but several other items did as well. It looked like Ashley had been in a rush when she'd snapped the pictures, and most of them were blurry. There was even a picture of her feet, for fuck's sake. Madison was tempted to call her again, but it would be useless. She'd sent him this email, and she'd know how he'd react when he got it. She'd call him as soon as she could and had cell service because she knew he'd freak out if she didn't.

Having gone through all the pictures, Madison finally turned his attention to the lines of text in the email. He frowned, then reread them.

I'm in trouble. I think I found the temple, but it's guarded. If you don't hear from me, they got me.

That was how the email ended. Ashley hadn't added any details, but the tone of the email was enough to tell Madison something wasn't right, and that was before considering the second sentence.

Had she found the temple? It looked like it from the pictures, but Madison couldn't be sure until he saw the place with his own eyes. He was worried about the bit where Ashley said the temple was guarded. Who was guarding it? Or maybe it was a *what*. And what did Ashley mean when she said that whoever guarded the temple might get her?

Madison told himself not to let his imagination run wild,

4

but it wasn't easy. He'd been looking for the temple since he was in college. The legends surrounding it and what it supposedly contained had been enough for him to want to find the place, and that was without even considering its the history. Madison had never been sure it actually existed, but he'd hoped.

And it seemed he'd been right.

If Ashley had found the temple, Madison needed to go. He didn't know how he'd manage with his job and everything else, but he'd find a way. This was what he'd been seeking for more than a decade. He wouldn't let anyone keep him away from the temple.

He couldn't afford to.

"It was a pleasure doing business with you," Ford told the man as they shook hands.

Mr. Johnson gave him a wide smile. "We'll contact you again if we ever come back to this corner of the world."

"You do that. I'll be waiting."

Ford wouldn't be. He doubted Mr. Johnson and his wife would ever come back, and even if they did, they'd probably have forgotten all about him by then. They'd got what they came for, and now they were going back to their everyday life, with their jobs and beautiful home, their kids, and whatnot. Ford had only listened with half an ear when Mrs. Johnson had told him about her family. He'd been more focused on the jungle and on making sure he didn't lose either of the spouses.

He doubted he'd have been paid if he had.

"Are you sure we can't invite you for dinner?" Mrs. Johnson said.

She was in her late fifties and always seemed to have a smile on her face. Ford didn't like a lot of people, but she'd been sweet, if talkative. Most people didn't worry for him, but she'd made sure he was eating and resting enough as they explored the jungle. She'd always had snacks on her, and she hadn't been shy about offering them to Ford, which was more than Ford could say for most of his clients.

"I'm sure," he said with a smile. He took her hand and lightly kissed the back of it. "You should focus on going back to your family. I'm sure they miss you fiercely."

Her cheeks flushed. "I suppose they do. Take care of yourself, Ford."

"I always do." If he didn't, he'd already be dead.

With one last wave, he left the Johnsons behind. He'd been paid handsomely for their week of exploring the jungle, and he couldn't wait to have a nice dinner. Maybe he'd even take a day off tomorrow. He couldn't remember the last time he'd allowed himself to relax, so it was probably about time.

"What the fuck are you doing here?" a man snarled.

Ford had been minding his own business and walking down the street, but he wasn't surprised that some members of his brother's pride had found him. He plastered a smile on his face, knowing he couldn't afford to start a fight, even though he was itching for one.

"Just going home," he said, keeping his tone calm.

"You stole our clients," a second voice said.

Great. Ford was being cornered not by one, not by two, but by three of his brother's pride members. Were they here to kick his ass, or did they just want to snarl at him for a bit? When it came to Diego's pride, it was anyone's guess, which was one of the reasons Ford refused to be part of it.

He raised his hands, hoping he was coming off as harmless. "I didn't know they were your clients. I don't want any trouble."

"Then you should leave town," Asshole One said.

"I'm afraid that won't be possible."

Asshole Three, who'd stayed silent until now, growled. For a moment, Ford wondered if he was going to have the balls to shift and attack him right there in the middle of the street. Diego wouldn't be happy if that happened, but Ford couldn't help but wonder what mattered the most to these people. They wanted to please their alpha, but maybe they wanted to kick Ford's ass more.

"Enough," a fourth person snapped.

Ford groaned. "I had everything in hand," he told his brother.

Diego stepped forward and crossed his massive arms over his chest. He glared at his three pride members, who clearly weren't here on his orders. The first two appeared cowed, but the third looked like he might still make a run for Ford.

Ford cracked his knuckles. He'd welcome the asshole if he tried.

"You know the rules," Diego said. "You leave my brother alone."

"Half-brother," Asshole Three said.

If looks could kill, he'd be taking his last breath just about now. Diego looked like he wanted to throttle him, which Ford understood. Some of his brother's pride members were kind of thick.

"He's my brother," Diego said. "That means that if you touch him, you touch me."

The threat in his voice was enough to finally get Asshole Three to take a step back. They all lightly bowed their head, which made Ford roll his eyes. Shifters could be a dramatic bunch in general, but his brother's pride took the cake.

"Go home," Diego ordered.

Thankfully, no one protested. Ford watched the three walk away and tried to do the same, even though he knew Diego wouldn't let him go easily.

"I'm sorry about that," Diego said before Ford could leave.

"Don't worry about it."

"How can I not? They have clear orders when it comes to you, and they keep disobeying."

Ford grinned. "That's because I'm such a likable guy. They want to spend more time with me."

"They'd be able to if you became a pride member."

"Not going to happen. Sorry, bro."

Diego grimaced. "You know I don't like it when you call me that."

"I'm not calling you Alpha."

"I don't expect you to, but you use that word too lightly. We *are* brothers, Ford, and that means a lot to me."

It meant a lot to Ford, too, but he'd never admit it out loud. "Whatever. I have to go. There's a steak calling my name, and I'm starving." Ford started to walk away, wondering if Diego would attempt to stop him. Sometimes his brother insisted they needed to talk, which usually ended in them bickering and getting frustrated.

"One day, you're going to have to stop running from this," Diego called out.

Ford waved without looking back. His brother wasn't wrong. Eventually, Ford would have to stop running.

But today wasn't the day.

CHAPTER TWO

Madison was filled with dread as he parked. He was the last one to arrive, which he'd done on purpose, even though it meant he'd have to walk up to the house. The driveway and the road in front of it were full of cars, which was enough to tell Madison that everyone was there.

His worst nightmare was coming true.

He stayed in his car, staring at the vehicles and wondering if he could get out of this. He didn't understand why his mother insisted he always come to family runs. A part of him knew it was because she wanted to act as if nothing was wrong, but he told himself it was also because she loved him. They were family, and she never purposefully tried to hurt him.

His parents had always felt guilty about him being what some people called the runt of the family. He'd been born prematurely, and he'd been tiny. He'd had many health problems as a newborn, but he'd gotten over them, and he was fine now. He'd just never grown much. His sister was taller than him, which wasn't hard, since he barely reached five foot four.

His height wasn't the only problem left behind by his premature arrival in this world. He could shift, but it always took him a bit longer. It didn't come as easy to him as it did to everyone else, which made family runs awkward. No one wanted to have to wait for him, and he hated when they all stared as he tried to be quick.

The front door opened, and his mother appeared. She looked right at him, which meant she'd seen him and that he wouldn't be able to come up with an excuse not to go in.

With a sigh, he got out of his car and locked it. His mother was back in the house by the time he reached the porch, and while he wanted nothing more than to turn around and make a run for it, he forced himself to go in. He'd grown up in this house, so he shouldn't feel as much dread as he did to be here.

The problem wasn't just his parents. Madison's mother was a lot on the best of days, and when Madison had to deal with her, he wanted nothing more than to run away and hide. She wasn't shy about the fact that his life wasn't what she'd wanted for him, and not just because he wasn't six foot four. He wasn't a doctor or a lawyer. He wasn't married, and even if he were, it wouldn't be to a woman. He didn't have kids.

A screech made him jump. He stepped to the side just in time to avoid two tiny wolf pups and a little girl chasing each other through the entrance. This family run would have been bad enough if it had only been his parents, his sister, and her family, but it looked like all the aunts, uncles, and cousins were there, too. It was almost like Thanksgiving, except everyone would shift except for Madison.

"Kill me now," he muttered as he made his way deeper inside the house.

There were kids everywhere he looked. Madison only had a sister, but the rest of the family was massive. His parents were the outliers when it came to having kids. Most of Madison's aunts and uncles had at least three kids, sometimes more. Of those kids, most had their own kids by now, and Madison wouldn't be surprised if the number of people in the house was close to fifty.

Fifty wolf shifters about to go outside and run together, leaving him behind to hold the fort and keep an eye on the food because they couldn't be bothered to wait for him. *Oh, what fun.*

"There you are," Lisa, Madison's sister, said.

She was holding a baby. She tried to get him to take it, but he quickly stepped back.

Lisa glared at him. "I've been holding this kid for half an hour. Allison keeps asking me when I'm going to have another, and I can't stand it."

"You tried telling her you're fine with only Peggy?"

"What do you think? It's why she dumped her youngest in my arms. She thinks he's going to make me want to have another kid or something."

Both Madison and Lisa rolled their eyes at the same time. That made Lisa grin, and Madison couldn't resist smiling back. He loved all of his family, but his favorite was his sister, now that their grandmother was gone. Neither of them had ever made him feel like he wasn't enough just because he had trouble with his shift.

Not that his parents did, at least not on purpose. Some of the things they said and did hurt, though, which was one of the reasons Madison spent as little time with them as he could.

"You could always run," Lisa said. "I'll tell Mom you had something urgent you forgot you needed to do."

"Like what?"

"I don't know. Student tests to correct or something? You're the smart guy, not me. You can come up with an excuse."

Madison bumped their shoulders together. "You're smart, too."

"I have good days, I guess. At least you see me as something more than a baby holder."

Allison had four kids, and she was known to dump them into the arms of anyone who stayed still long enough. Madison and Lisa's cousin didn't seem to care that sometimes those people didn't want to hold her child. Lisa had been her victim in this case, but Madison had been in her place before. He'd learned to avoid Allison so he wouldn't have to hold a baby.

Lisa leaned closer. "She's pregnant again," she whispered, tilting her chin at the baby so Madison could tell who she was talking about.

"When is she going to stop? Do you think we should tell her husband to buy a TV for their bedroom?"

Lisa barked out a laugh. "We could certainly try."

"What are the two of you whispering about?" their mother said, appearing in the entrance.

"Nothing," Madison said quickly. He didn't want her to start poking around.

"Then you can come and help me." She looked at Lisa. "You look good with a baby in your arms. You should think about it."

Madison went over to hug his mom. He didn't want her and Lisa to start bickering, and distracting their mom was the best way to keep them apart. He winked at his sister, and she smiled gratefully. It wouldn't stop their mother from insisting she needed to give Peggy a younger sibling, but at least for now, Lisa was safe.

Madison was not.

"And what about you?" his mother asked as she pulled him deeper into the house. "When are you going to make me a grandmother?"

"Lisa has already done that. You don't need me to make you a grandmother." Madison was glad Lisa had a kid, because he wasn't planning on having any. He knew better than to tell his mother that, especially when the house was full of family members.

"Maybe not, but it would be nice to have kids from you, too. I can already see them, with their messy hair and glasses. You were adorable as a child."

That might be true, but Madison wasn't a child anymore. He was far from adorable, with his graying brown hair and the stomach that would never vanish, no matter how many times he told himself it was time to get on a diet.

Thankfully, with so many people in the house, Madison's mother was quickly distracted. He took advantage of that and hid in a corner, watching the family and feeling like he was on the outside of everything.

He supposed he was. He was here, but he wouldn't be running with the family. Most people didn't even notice him during the family runs because they were so focused on having fun that he might as well not be there. It had been that way since he was a child. He'd been different, and while the adults had either pitied him or ignored him, his cousins had been cruel and had teased him endlessly about his height.

Tonight wasn't any different. Once everyone had arrived, Madison's mother guided the family to the back porch. She didn't even notice that Madison didn't follow. What would be the point? He didn't want to make a spectacle of himself, and no one would care that he wasn't there. He didn't exactly avoid shifting, but he only did so when he was alone and when his wolf was threatening to take over if he didn't, which never ended well.

Madison stayed hidden in the corner of the living room, peering out the window as everyone stripped and shifted, even the babies — who were faster at shifting than Madison could ever be, even though they couldn't walk in their human form yet. Their mothers were there to help them to their feet, and sure enough, Allison's stomach was distended. It was much more obvious in her wolf form than in her human form.

Madison sighed and pressed his forehead against the cool glass of the window. His father threw his head up and howled at the moon, and everyone followed suit.

Everyone except Madison, who watched them run into the forest behind the house while he stayed behind.

Ford smiled at the knock on his door because he knew exactly who it was. He'd recognized the footsteps as she came closer to the door, and since he didn't want her to stand on her feet for too long, he quickly got up from the couch and went to open it.

"I knew I'd heard you," Ford's neighbor, Mrs. Garcia, said. She pushed a plate into his hands. "I cooked you dinner."

"Thank you, but you didn't have to." He always protested when she brought food over, and she always waved him off. It was how they did things, and it never failed to make Ford smile.

"If I don't cook you dinner, you'd only eat bad things."

Madison wouldn't call the steak he'd had last night a bad thing, but he knew what she meant. It hadn't been home cooked.

He took the plate from her hands and stepped aside, but she shook her head. "I don't have time to come in tonight."

"Oh? Do you have a date?"

"In fact, I do. And before you say anything, I made sure he was a gentleman before saying yes. You don't have to threaten him."

Madison nodded, satisfied. "As long as he treats you right, he has nothing to fear from me."

He was protective of his neighbor. Mrs. Garcia was in her seventies, yet, she had a busier social life than Ford. She found it funny, and while Ford was amused, it was how he liked things. He'd always been a loner and couldn't see that changing anytime soon. When he needed to scratch an itch, he found a guy in a club or bar, got what he needed, then went back to being a loner. It was what worked for him and what made Mrs. Garcia desperate. She wanted to see Ford settle down and didn't care that he liked guys. She just wanted him to be loved.

"Do you need anything before I go?" she asked.

Ford should be the one asking that. He'd been trying to take care of her since he'd realized her family never visited. A few members lived far away, so he could understand, but one of her sons lived only a few streets over. Ford was always tempted to visit the guy and introduce him to his fist after he spent some time with Mrs. Garcia, but what would be the point? He couldn't force anyone to care about their mother. After all, he didn't care for his, so much so that he'd run back to his father's country even though he'd never been close to that side of his family.

Mrs. Garcia was nothing like Ford's mother. She was the caring grandmother type, and she'd adopted him. She treated him like a grandson, which he enjoyed, and he never wanted her to get hurt. That was why he talked to her dates to make sure they treated her right. He couldn't wait for the time when Mrs. Garcia met her soulmate. He'd be happy not to have to keep an eye on her anymore.

She reached out and patted Ford's cheek. "I have to go now. Be good."

"Always."

"We both know that's a lie, but I want to believe it for tonight."

Ford was still laughing as he closed the door. He stayed there, peeking through the window to make sure Mrs. Garcia got into her apartment all right. It was just next door, but he always checked.

Once her door was closed behind her, Ford sighed and took the plate to the kitchen. He wasn't hungry yet, but he would be later today, and he was happy he wouldn't have to attempt to cook. The way Mrs. Garcia took care of him warmed his heart, and he couldn't help but wonder if this was what life would be like if he agreed to become a member of his brother's pride.

Would they take care of him? Would they worry about him not eating?

He huffed. It was no use worrying over it. He'd never be a member of Diego's pride, and that was how he wanted things. He was perfectly fine on his own.

Or at least, that was what he tried to convince himself of.

Madison was ready to leave the second his family started coming back from the run. He had things to do, including planning a trip to a foreign country and a stay in the jungle. Usually, when he worked over the summer, he divided his time between hotels and the jungle, with a definite preference for soft beds and running water. Ashley had a room in the hotel they usually used, and Madison hoped to find her there, but something was wrong. The end of the email was proof of that, and Madison couldn't help but wonder what would happen if he had to fight his way to Ashley.

Nothing good.

His mother walked into the kitchen, and he got to his feet. "I'm going to go," he told her.

She frowned. "Why? And why weren't you out there with us?"

"Do you really have to ask?"

His mother stared at him for a moment. "We try to include you. You always say you feel like you don't matter to us, but that's not true. I asked you to come for the run, didn't I? But instead of spending time with us, you hid in the kitchen. You're the one who didn't make an effort, not us."

Madison remembered that conversation. She'd *ordered* him to come, although she'd hidden it in pretty words and pleases.

"What did you think would happen?" Madison was frustrated. It wasn't the first time she told him to come to the family run, and it probably wouldn't be the last. Madison's mother was as stubborn as they came, and she couldn't see how much she was hurting him.

Yes, Madison often felt like he didn't matter to most of his family because of the way they'd treated him since he was a child. That didn't mean that asking him to come to a family run would change anything. In fact, it made him feel even more like an outsider, and he despised it.

"What do you want me to do?" his mother asked. "Maybe you should see the doctors again. I heard about a new one a few towns over. We could go and see what he says."

Madison was already shaking his head. "I can't."

"Why not? There has to be a way to help you control your shift better. There's nothing wrong with you."

Maybe she was right, but Madison didn't care anymore. He'd made his peace with himself and his problems, or at least he'd made his peace with the fact that no doctor could help him any more than they already had.

But he didn't need to change to be whole. He didn't need to shift faster to be loved.

That was the way things should be, but the only person beyond his sister who'd never tried to get him to change and who'd never seen anything wrong with him was his grandmother, and she'd died a few years before. Since then, Madison had felt more alone than ever, and no family run would change that. His family would never change. They'd always want him to be different, but he was who he was, and he wasn't going to change in the hope they'd love him.

He didn't say that out loud. His mother hadn't been happy when he'd decided to study history or when he'd told her he was going to teach. She'd hoped he would become a doctor or maybe a lawyer, something she could use to make herself feel important when she was with her friends. She was already at a disadvantage because Madison wasn't good-looking and had trouble shifting. She felt it was her fault since he'd been born early because she'd fallen off a ladder while painting his nursery.

Since she felt that way, she'd always tried to push Madison to be better, or at least a version of himself she thought would be better. He should talk to the doctors to find a way to shift more easily. He should become a doctor or a lawyer so he'd be wealthy.

Instead, she had to tell people that not only was he a damaged shifter, but he also taught shifter history at a college.

The horror.

"There has to be someone out there who can find out why you're the way you are and help you," she insisted.

Madison could hear the sound of more people coming inside the house. They were excited and happy, probably exhausted, too. Now that the run was over, they'd all gather to eat more food, and Madison had no intention of sticking around for that. He'd done his part. He'd come to the run, and he'd stood by and watched as his family disappeared into the forest to run and play. He'd listened to them howl and call to each other.

And he hadn't been part of it. He hadn't wanted to be.

"I don't have time to do any of this right now," he told his mother because she wouldn't let it go otherwise. "I'm leaving the country."

She frowned. "What are you talking about?"

"I'm going back to the jungle. I got an email from Ashley, and she found something."

"You only go to the jungle during the summer."

"Because I have my job. I can't stand by and let this go, though. Ashley needs me."

Madison's mother frowned. "But you told me the two of you aren't together."

Madison almost groaned. "She's my friend. We don't need to be together for me to worry about her."

"Surely she doesn't expect you to drop everything and go

to her just because she's found something. You always find stuff when you're there for the summer."

She wasn't wrong. Just this summer, Madison had found several pieces of pottery. His family didn't understand how exciting it was. Not many people did. To them, they were just dirty and broken bits and pieces. To Madison, they were a sign of the people who had lived there and who were long gone. He wanted to find out more about them, and he wanted to find the temple.

He wasn't about to tell his mother why. He hadn't told anyone, not even Ashley. She thought he was interested in the temple for the same reasons she was — it was a precious testimony of the past that people needed to know about. "Well, I have to go."

"You can't. Thanksgiving is just around the corner, and I've already invited most of the family. I'm hosting this year."

That meant Madison would have to be careful not to be back in time. "I promise I'll be back by then," he lied.

"You can't just drop everything just because your friend needs you," his mother protested. "Besides, didn't you tell me that the guide you usually use retired?"

That *was* going to be a problem, and Madison would have to find a solution, but he'd have to wait until he was there. The best guides were local, and most of them didn't use email or anything like that. "I'll find another one," he told his mother as he inched closer to the door. "I'll be fine. I don't want you to worry if you don't hear from me. You know cell phone service isn't great in the jungle."

"I also know the jungle is dangerous. You can't even shift right. What are you going to do if an animal attacks you? You won't be able to shift in time to defend yourself."

Even though she made this argument every year, Madison bristled at what she was implying. "I'm not weak," he said through gritted teeth.

"I never said you were weak. I'm just worried about you because you don't have the same advantages other shifters have."

"I'll be fine." He had to convince himself of that, because otherwise, he'd never go. "I don't want you to worry about me."

"You're my son, and I worry about you. I don't want you to go."

Because she didn't understand how important it was. Even if Madison didn't have wild hopes that the temple could help him get back the most important person in his life, he'd still go because he'd been working toward this for years, reading dusty books and journals, digging in the jungle, and lecturing bored students. It was his job, a big part of his life, and his passion. To his mother, it might only be dirty old stone, but to Madison, it was a peek into a world that was long gone. He'd always been fascinated with how people had lived before, and finding the temple would give him an insight into that.

It would take him away from his family during Thanksgiving and possibly Christmas, which was a bonus.

"I'm going, and it's non-negotiable. I'll be back as soon as possible."

Madison turned, ready to go. His mother wouldn't let him leave if he didn't push, and he wasn't up to listening to her rant for hours about how he wouldn't have to travel during the holidays if he'd just become a doctor.

"Madison!" his mother called out.

He didn't turn. He'd told her where he was going and what would happen, and he wouldn't let her stop him. He didn't want her to worry, but he could admit at least to himself that finding the temple and Ashley was more important than making his mother happy.

Making himself happy was a bonus.

Chapter Three

As always, the first thing that hit Madison when he stepped out of the plane was the heat. He'd hoped that coming during fall meant he wouldn't have to deal with as much of it, but he'd been wrong. It was hot as hell, even though it was November.

He was already sweating by the time he grabbed his luggage and left the airport. Being outside made him want to turn around and go straight back to the plane, but he told himself that Ashley needed him. He'd tried calling her several times, emailed, and called her family, but no one had heard from her. It was like she'd vanished from the surface of the earth right after emailing him, and Madison was worried.

But he had a plan. He grabbed a cab and headed to the hotel. He knew what room she was in, and hopefully, it wouldn't be a problem to get into it. They always used the same hotel when they came for the summer and were friendly with most of the people who worked there.

Madison wasn't sure what he'd do after getting there. It would depend on what he'd find, but he had every intention of bringing Ashley home. He couldn't even think about what might have happened to her. As far as he was concerned, she was perfectly fine, and he'd find her soon. Maybe she'd been so focused on the new finds that she'd forgotten to email him back. Maybe she'd lost her phone, which would explain why it went straight to voicemail.

That had to be it. Madison refused to consider any other option, like Ashley being hurt — or worse.

After giving the driver the hotel address, he settled in the back of the cab. He watched the city go by through the window, his mind already working on his next step.

He wanted to go to the temple, but Ashley hadn't given him the coordinates. He had plenty of pictures but no idea where the temple was, although he could take a few guesses. He and Ashley had been exploring a specific part of the forest before he had to go back to his day job. She hadn't mentioned moving on, which meant that was where she'd found the temple. She'd had to come back to the city to email Madison, so whatever happened to her happened here. Madison could probably avoid going to the temple, but he had the feeling that whatever was going on with Ashley was because of the ruins.

He also desperately wanted to explore them and find out whether or not they could cure him.

Everyone knew the legend here. Long ago, a shifter pride had lived in the area. They didn't hide from humans and lived peacefully with them until the missionaries arrived. To them, shifters weren't normal people who could turn into animals but monsters. They'd been afraid, and eventually, they'd pushed the pride into the forest, where they'd vanished, never to be seen again. There were rumors that the pride still lived there, but Madison had never seen anyone, even though he'd been poking around the jungle for a few years now.

He'd also never found the temple, so anything was possible.

The stories around the temple were wild. Most of them involved magic and incredible powers, which made Madison suspect magic was involved in how a shifter was able to shift, which might explain why no doctor had ever been able to help him. There were studies about it, but it wasn't his area of expertise. The temple was, though, and he was planning to explore it as soon as he found Ashley.

He was relieved when he got to the hotel. The air conditioning inside made it easier to breathe, and he took a few seconds to relax right next to the door. He could feel the sweat drying on his skin, but he didn't have time to linger.

He had Ashley's room number, so he didn't stop at the front desk. He could come back downstairs once he was sure she wasn't in the room. He didn't want to attract too much attention in case she was fine and had simply forgotten to email him back.

After getting turned around a few times because all the hallways and doors looked the same, Madison found the right door. A *Do not disturb* sign was hanging from the handle, but when he tried to open the door, he found it wasn't locked. He gently pushed the door open and poked his head in. "Ashley?"

He didn't have to go in to know she wouldn't be there. One look at the room was enough to tell him that.

It was trashed. The room was small, but with everything on the floor, it looked even smaller. The bed had been stripped of its sheets and the mattress pushed to the floor as if someone had thought Ashley would be hiding something under it. The small desk by the window had been crowded with Ashley's computers and notes the last time Madison had been here, but everything was on the floor now.

Well, almost everything. From where he was, Madison couldn't see Ashley's computer. It was clear that whoever had done this had taken it, but he couldn't tell if they'd stolen anything else. Even if they hadn't, Ashley was nowhere to be seen, and Madison was starting to freak out.

He closed the door again, left his bags by the door, and rushed downstairs. There was no line at the front desk, and the young woman behind it smiled at him when she saw him.

"How can I help you?"

"I need you to call the police," Madison told her.

She blinked, and her smile faltered. "I'm sorry? Why do I need to call the police?"

"I'm here to see my friend. She's in room one three seven, but when I went there, I found the door open and the room trashed. She's not there and hasn't been answering her phone."

The woman paled. "Let me call my supervisor."

Madison needed her to call the police, not her supervisor, but he didn't snap at her. It wasn't her fault that something had happened to Ashley. She was understandably confused, but Madison supposed anyone would be in her place.

A man came in through a door behind the front desk. He gave Madison a tight smile before leaning over the woman and talking to her in a soothing voice. She kept peeking at Madison, and Madison had to resist the urge to glare. Didn't they understand that something had happened to Ashley?

"Can you tell me what the problem is, sir?" The supervisor said.

The name tag on his chest told Madison his name was Antonio. "I'm here to visit a friend, and I found her room trashed. She's nowhere to be found and hasn't been answering her phone in days." Madison didn't say he suspected Ashley had been taken. He knew how ridiculous that would sound, and he needed Antonio to do something about Ashley's disappearance, not laugh in his face.

"Can you give me more details, like your friend's name?"

Madison obeyed. He watched as Antonio poked around on the computer for a moment. Something about him made Madison's skin crawl, but he told himself to ignore it.

"She left a note saying that she was visiting the small towns in the area and would be gone for a few weeks," Antonio said. "It looks like she didn't warn you."

That wasn't possible. Ashley was here to work, not to be a tourist. Besides, there was the email. Madison was sure something had happened to her, and there was no way she would have left that note.

What was going on? Why was this guy involved? It was the only explanation that made sense. That note hadn't come from Ashley, but someone had entered it into the computer, and Madison was ready to bet it had been Antonio.

Which meant the man might be dangerous. Madison was freaking out, but he told himself he couldn't show it. So he plastered a smile on his lips and nodded. "I see. Well, that complicates things. I don't have two weeks to wait for her, but I'm here, so I might as well explore the city, right?"

Antonio's shoulders slumped in what Madison was sure was relief. He wanted to punch him, but instead, he smiled like an idiot. People tended to underestimate him, which always played in his favor. He wanted that to happen today, too.

"Have you booked a room with us?"

"I'm afraid I haven't, but I'd like to stay in Ashley's room if it's possible." Antonio hesitated, and Madison was pretty sure he was about to say no. He couldn't allow that to happen. "It's not like she's using the room at the moment, and we were planning on sharing anyway," he said with a smile. "Or I suppose I could call the police. I don't think they'd be happy, but I'd feel better."

"I'll give you a second key to the room," Antonio quickly said.

If he was involved, Madison would find out, and if something had happened to Ashley, he'd make Antonio pay for it.

But first, he had to find her, and that wasn't going to be easy.

Ford liked this hotel, which was why he tended to hang around the bar as often as he could. It was the best way to find clients, and the beer was cold, good, and cheap.

He took another sip as he idly listened to the conversations around him. Every time he spotted tourists, he turned his attention to them. He'd been a guide long enough that he could tell with a glance when someone was a tourist and when they were here for business. Most of the tourists were focused on exploring the city, but some enjoyed nature and wanted to see more of the jungle, and that was where Ford stepped in.

"Let the alpha know," someone close by said, getting Ford's attention.

He discreetly glanced around until he found the person who'd mentioned their alpha. The man had to work for the hotel, since he wore a uniform, and Ford was pretty sure he'd seen him before. Was this guy one of Diego's pride members? Ford didn't know most of them. He'd been taken away when he was very young, and after he'd come back, he hadn't been planning on making friends within the pride. They were everywhere, though, so he wasn't surprised that one of them worked here.

"I will," the man the hotel guy was talking to promised. "Why do you think he's here?"

"Because of the temple. Why else? Just let the alpha know what's going on. He asked for a guide, so it would be better if the pride could provide him with one. That way, we can keep an eye on him and ensure he doesn't poke his nose in areas he should stay away from."

The second man nodded. "Find someone. We need to take care of him like we did the woman."

Ford's stomach churned. Whatever they were talking about, it didn't sound good. He didn't want to believe his brother would hurt a woman, but he didn't really know Diego. Besides, as the alpha, Diego's main job was to keep his pride safe. If that meant getting rid of a few people, Ford doubted anything would stop his brother.

Ford wanted to ask Diego, but he couldn't reach out to him. That meant he'd have to find another way to keep this guy safe, whoever he was. From what the hotel guy had said, the guy was here for some temple. If the pride had already disposed of a woman, they wouldn't hesitate to get rid of this guy if he got too nosy.

Ford tapped his fingertips on the bar. It was none of his business, and he wasn't a pride member. He didn't care about someone getting hurt because he didn't know them—he didn't like the idea, but he didn't care. What he did care about was the temple. Where was it? Could Ford earn money from it?

The hotel guy had said that the man was looking for a guide, so maybe he was ready to try to find this temple. That was going to be Ford's entry point. The man needed a guide, and Ford happened to be one. He could give him whatever he needed.

Or at least, he hoped so.

Whatever guide the hotel guy found would be part of the pride. Ford had no doubt about that, and he wasn't going to stick around to find out for sure. Usually, guides met their clients at their hotels, so Ford would just have to get here before the pride guide did.

"Excuse me," a man said.

The hotel guy and the other one turned to look at him. Ford did the same, albeit more discreetly.

"That's him," the hotel guy said in a whisper. "I'll keep an eye on him while you warn the alpha."

Ford stared at the man hovering nearby, watching the hotel guy. He looked nothing like what Ford had expected. The people who wanted to explore the jungle usually knew what they were doing. Not all of them could keep up with the physical aspect of it, but there was no way in hell this guy had any idea what he was doing.

He was wearing a pair of shorts and a short-sleeved shirt. He looked to be in his mid to late thirties, with brown hair that had started graying on the sides. Ford couldn't see what color his eyes were, but he was wearing glasses that he kept pushing up his nose, and the shirt he wore revealed that he was a little round and probably didn't spend a lot of time in the gym.

Exactly Ford's type, although that wasn't something Ford was going to consider.

"Mr. Williams?" the hotel guy asked in a smarmy voice.

"I wanted to talk to you about that guide."

"I'll be happy to find someone for you, although I'll need more details."

"There's nothing to say. I want to explore the forest and find a place my friend told me about. The guy I would normally use retired, which is why I need a new one."

"I'll find you someone for tomorrow. Is that soon enough?"

"It should be fine."

Ford listened as the two spoke. He took quick notes on his phone, just in case. He didn't want to forget anything the man was saying, especially because he'd need to be fast and smart about this.

He had to reach Mr. Williams early tomorrow before the pride could get to him. He'd tell him he was the guide the hotel had found for him and whisk him away before the pride realized what he'd done. It would be a lie, but Ford wasn't bothered by lying. He did it often, and he was good at it.

He had no idea what was happening, but whatever it was, he didn't like the sound of it. If his brother had made a woman disappear, Ford didn't want to be involved, so he'd stay away from the pride like he always did.

For now, he could focus on Mr. Williams and how deliciously adorable he was. Ford wasn't in this for sex, but he couldn't deny he wouldn't say no if Mr. Williams were to climb into his bed.

But Ford was in this because he needed to survive, and finding whatever temple Mr. Williams was looking for could get both of them a lot of money, even more so if Ford somehow managed to get the location of the temple from Mr. Williams and then left him behind.

This wasn't going to be fun, but it would be lucrative.

CHAPTER FOUR

Madison was nervous. He hadn't thought about it yesterday when asking Antonio for a guide, but what would happen if Antonio was involved with Ashley's disappearance? If Antonio had hurt Ashley, would he want to hurt Madison, too? Madison was asking questions, which probably wasn't something Antonio wanted. It would be too easy for someone to take Madison to the jungle, leave him there, or even kill him. No one would know what had happened to him. It would be a small miracle if someone even found his body.

But he didn't want to think about bodies because he'd start wondering if Ashley was dead if he did. That wasn't something he wanted to consider, so he finished getting ready. He'd already packed his backpack, so he grabbed it as soon as he was done, ready for whatever the day would throw at him. He locked the hotel room door behind himself, although Antonio could easily get in if he wanted to. Madison hadn't left anything around that would point to why he was here beyond tourism, and he hoped Antonio would believe it. He just might, as long as he had nothing to do with Ashley's disappearance.

It was still early, so there weren't many people around when Madison reached the hotel entrance. Even the front desk was empty, and he looked around for someone to ask about the guide. He didn't particularly want to talk to Antonio, so he hoped he wasn't around this early in the morning. He poked his head into the dining room, hoping that if his guide was already here, they'd stopped to get something to eat.

There were a few people at the tables in the dining room. Madison dismissed the elderly couple, as well as the family of four. That only left one person sitting alone, and while the man might not be Madison's guide, he was still a sight to behold.

Madison wasn't here to have a one-night stand, but he couldn't deny this man was handsome and someone he might have been interested in at home. He was more than a little rusty when it came to flirting, though, so he probably wouldn't have attempted anything even in a normal situation.

Even though the man was seated, Madison could tell he was tall. His long legs were stretched out in front of him under the table, and his dark hair flopped in front of his forehead. He pushed it away and took a sip of what was probably coffee. Then he looked up, and his dark eyes met Madison's.

Madison sucked in a breath. He couldn't smell the man, but he was pretty sure he was a shifter, possibly a big cat, from the way he moved as he got up from his chair. He was graceful enough for that to be so, anyway.

"Mr. Williams?" the man asked.

Madison blinked at him. He knew his name, so he had to be the guide.

The man smiled. It made him look gentler, but Madison couldn't ignore the wariness in his expression.

"Yes, I'm Mr. Williams. Madison, I mean."

The man's smile widened. "My name is Ford Owens. I'm here to be your guide in the jungle today."

So he *was* Madison's guide. Was he working with Antonio? It didn't look like it, but what did Madison know? He had no idea who this guy was. Ford might have something to do with Ashley's disappearance, but Madison couldn't be sure, and he didn't want to make accusations when he didn't have proof.

Ford looked around. "We should head out. The sooner we get to the jungle, the better it will be. It's not too hot at the moment, but that will change."

Madison groaned. He was already sweating, dammit. "Did you really have to remind me of that?"

"Well, I thought you should know. Is this your first time exploring the jungle?"

"It's not."

Ford didn't look convinced. He probably thought Madison was a liar, and Madison couldn't blame him. He didn't look like he did a lot of walking around jungles. The only physical activity he did was during the summer when he was here. Once he was back home, he was so focused on his job and everything else that he barely had time for the gym. Besides, he didn't particularly enjoy having to exercise in front of others. No one had ever said anything to him, but he knew when he was being judged.

He hiked up his backpack higher on his shoulder and nodded. "We can go whenever you want."

Ford looked around again, then ushered Madison out of the dining room in a way that made Madison wonder if he was trying to run without paying for his breakfast. The only thing that had been on the table was coffee, though, so it didn't make much sense.

"Before we go anywhere, I feel like I should ask you how much you want to be paid," Madison said, digging in his heels.

He didn't know what was happening, but he could tell Ford was trying to get him away from the hotel as quickly as possible. Was this what he'd done to Ashley, too? Or was he innocent of what had happened to her?

"We can talk about that once we're in the jungle," Ford reassured him.

"No. I'd rather talk about it here."

"Are you afraid I'll leave you out there?"

"You could. This might not be my first visit, but it doesn't mean I can find my way out without a guide. So are you available to spend, let's say, a week in the jungle with me?"

Ford cocked his head. "That long?"

"To begin with." They'd have to come back after a week, possibly sooner. Madison didn't have a lot of food in his backpack, and he couldn't see Ford's bag anywhere.

Ford's gaze flickered to something behind Madison. Madison started to turn to see what it was, but Ford grabbed his wrist and pulled him along. "We can stay a week," Ford confirmed.

"What are you doing? Why are you dragging me away from the hotel?"

Madison stopped moving, but Ford was strong. That wasn't a surprise, considering the muscles moving under his t-shirt, but Madison couldn't afford to be distracted.

"I apologize," Ford said. "I just want to start right away. My car is just around the corner."

"You're behaving strangely." It wasn't the best idea to follow Ford to his car. Something was definitely up with him, and Madison had no way of knowing if it was because of Ashley or because of something else.

Ford suddenly stopped and turned to face Madison. "I apologize. If I can be honest, I didn't expect you to be the kind of person who wants to explore the jungle. I suppose I'm afraid you'll change your mind, and I need your money to survive."

Madison softened. He wanted to believe that was the only reason Ford was so frantic. "I promise I'll pay you, and I'm not changing my mind. We're going into the jungle."

Ford grinned at him, then reached around him to open a car door. Their bodies brushed against each other, and now,

Madison was close enough to be sure that Ford was a shifter.

He couldn't tell what kind of shifter, but it didn't matter. He didn't want Ford to realize that he was a shifter, too, so he quickly stepped away. He stumbled back, falling into the passenger seat of the car. Ford took advantage, quickly closing the door before Madison could do or say anything. Madison struggled to get into a better position, and by the time he was sitting upright in the seat, Ford was in the driver's seat and starting the car.

"We still need to talk about how much you want to be paid," Madison said.

"We can talk about that on the way. Better get an early start, don't you think?"

"There's an early start, and there's this," Madison grumbled.

He couldn't trust Ford, but he didn't need to. Madison would be careful in case Ford was working with Antonio, and if he was, then Madison would find a way to get away from him. He wanted to find Ashley, and he suspected that she might be somewhere around the temple, since her disappearance was linked to it.

This was the first step in Madison's search for Ashley and the temple.

So why did it feel more like he was being kidnapped?

As Ford drove off, he glanced at the entrance of the hotel. He'd panicked when he'd seen the two guys from the hotel yesterday step out of the hotel. The one who wasn't wearing a hotel uniform wore clothes that wouldn't be out of place in the jungle, comfortable looking and sturdy. He had to be the guide chosen for Madison, which meant Ford was running out of time to convince Madison to come with him. Madison was understandably wary and hesitant, but Ford could be charming, and he was pretty sure he could get Madison to follow him.

Madison hadn't mentioned anything about the temple, just that he wanted to stay in the jungle for about a week. Ford would have been surprised if he hadn't known what Madison was looking for, but he did and had half a mind of finding the temple on his own. Madison was the only one who knew the area where the temple was, though. That meant they'd have to stick together, which, in turn, meant that Ford would have to be careful about when he dumped Madison.

"I'm not sure how I feel about this," Madison said, looking around the car as he wrinkled his nose.

Ford would be the first to admit his car wasn't great. It was little more than a rust bucket, and he wouldn't be surprised if it died on him someday soon. Ford needed enough money to get another car, and the temple would give him that.

If they ever got there.

"What are you looking for in the jungle?" he asked. He was curious about Madison. Contrary to Ford, he didn't seem like someone who was in this for the money.

"Who said I was looking for something?"

"I don't know. It's odd that you want to spend an entire week in the jungle for no reason."

"Why do your clients usually spend time in the jungle?"

Madison had Ford there. The people he took to the jungle enjoyed it most of the time. Sometimes, they just wanted to be able to brag that they'd been there and had lived rough for a week. Those were the exceptions, though. The others enjoyed sleeping on the ground and exploring something that was nothing more than trees, trees, and more trees.

Well, and the temple, but it was well hidden.

Ford had never found it in all the times he'd explored the forest. He'd been there dozens of times, both in his human and jaguar forms. He was surprised he hadn't been able to locate it, especially when he was shifted. He supposed he needed to know where to look, which was where Madison came in.

Ford had heard the legends, like everyone in the area. The pride had built the temple hundreds of years ago when they still mingled with humans without hiding who they were. They hadn't used it since the missionaries had arrived, and the pride had taken a step away from humans and had entered a life of secrecy they still upheld now. They didn't live in the jungle anymore, but unlike most shifters in the world, they weren't outspoken about being shifters. The temple was a sacred place to them, and Ford had never been allowed there, not even when he was a child. Back then, he'd been a pride member, but he'd been looked at like he was different.

Probably because he was. His mother had made sure of that, and while he'd always be angry at her for taking him away, he also understood why she had. It couldn't have been easy for her to live here when most of the pride looked at her like she was a stranger.

And she had been. She'd been American, not local. Ford and Diego's father had fallen in love with her, and she'd moved here. It hadn't been what she expected, though, and when Ford was a kid, she'd moved them back to the US. He'd lost his father, and even though he hadn't felt part of the pride, it was the only family he'd ever known. Back in the States, he and his mother had been alone. That was why when she died, Ford had come back.

He'd thought he'd find a home, but he'd been wrong. No one had welcomed him back except maybe Diego, but Ford didn't know what to do with him, which was one of the reasons he decided to stay away. He didn't want anything to do with the pride after the way they'd treated him and his mother.

Yet he was trying to find their temple. They were going to

be pissed when they realized he was involved, and Diego wouldn't be able to protect him this time. It was almost enough for him to take a step back.

Almost.

"I don't like any of this," Madison grumbled. "It feels like you're kidnapping me."

Ford chuckled. "You'd know it if I were kidnapping you."

"Would I?"

Ford needed to keep Madison happy. He was the only one who could guide him to the temple, and Ford needed whatever was hidden there to survive.

Or at least, that was what he told himself. His brother would be pissed when he found out about this, but Ford couldn't afford to care. He and Diego had never been close, so it wouldn't matter anyway. As long as he stayed out of the way of the pride, nothing would come out of it.

Except that Diego would be hurt. Ford knew what he was doing, and he was going to do it anyway. It wouldn't endear him to his brother, but Ford wasn't worried about that.

His survival came first, and Diego wasn't part of that. Hell, he was barely even part of Ford's life.

And Ford intended to keep it that way.

CHAPTER FIVE

Madison was still annoyed an hour later when Ford finally stopped the car. He looked around, trying to identify the small town in which they'd stopped. The jungle wasn't close to the city where the hotel was, which meant driving until they reached it. That was one of the reasons Madison needed a guide, but he didn't know what to make of Ford.

The man had been silent the entire way. Madison had grumbled, but he was afraid to be too obvious about what he suspected Ford's role in this was. There was no way Ford wasn't involved, and it was scary. Madison didn't know what had happened to Ashley or what might happen to him. He didn't know anything for sure except that the temple was somewhere in the jungle, and the excitement was enough to push him to get out of the car.

He stretched and looked at where Ford had parked. They were in front of a tiny bar, and Ford was already on his way inside. Madison wasn't sure he should follow. The bar had seen better days, and it looked like it might crumble if too many people walked into it. It tilted heavily to the side and was incredibly dirty, and Madison had no plans of dying anytime soon.

But Ford turned, a smile on his lips. "Are you coming?"

"Only if I want to die," Madison grumbled, but he did follow Ford.

For some reason, the man was still smiling. He seemed to do that a lot, which puzzled Madison. If Ford was here to kill him, why was he so relaxed? Why hadn't he stopped the car on the side of the road when they'd been alone for miles and done what he needed to do? It would have been easy, but instead, he was going along with what Madison wanted. He'd driven Madison all the way here, and it looked like he might actually want to guide Madison through the jungle.

"We need to get supplies if we're going to stay in there for a week," Ford declared as he pushed open the door and stepped aside to let Madison in.

Madison had to brush against his body, and he couldn't repress the shiver that ran down his spine. So close he could smell Ford, and it confirmed Ford was a shifter. Madison wasn't planning to tell Ford he was one, though. He wasn't going to shift in the jungle, so there was no point telling him.

The temple had been sacred to the original pride who'd lived in the area. No one knew when they'd built it, but it was a long time ago. Hopefully, Madison would find more details about their lives and what had happened to them after they'd vanished into the jungle once he was able to explore the ruins. He was interested in the place for its history as well as for its magic. He'd need time to look around and take notes and a ton of pictures.

The problem was that he didn't know if that was possible. The pride had been secretive since the missionaries had started messing things up for them. They'd retreated to the jungle, and they'd disappeared. There were rumors that the pride was still around, but Madison found that hard to believe. He hoped he was wrong, because if he wasn't, the pride wouldn't be happy about him poking his nose around their sacred temple.

But he needed the magic of the temple. If it was real, it could help him get his grandmother back, and that was all he'd wanted since he'd lost her. She was the reason he'd first become interested in history and had started exploring this part of the world. It had been her passion, but she'd grown up in a different time and hadn't been allowed to follow it. Instead, she'd gotten married and had children. She'd never stopped loving history, though, and some of Madison's fondest memories were of her telling him and his sister about magical temples and long-lost shifters.

"So, what do we need to buy?" Ford asked, pulling Madison out of his thoughts.

"You're the guide. You tell me."

Ford arched a brow. "It would be easier if I knew what you wanted to do in the forest."

Madison crossed his arms over his chest and glared. "I already told you that. I just enjoy walking around and looking at the trees and animals."

Ford stared at Madison for a moment. It was clear he didn't believe him, and Madison wondered if he knew about the temple. He wasn't about to ask, and he was relieved when Ford let it go.

"All right," he said with a smile. "One week of getting bitten by mosquitoes and sleeping on the hard ground coming up."

Madison rolled his eyes. He knew it wouldn't be easy. It never was. He couldn't back down, though, and he wouldn't allow anyone to stop him.

Madison watched with wide eyes as Ford went up to the bartender and got himself a shot of something. It wasn't what Madison had expected, but then, this was a bar. He looked around, and sure enough, there were no signs of the supplies they'd need for the week ahead of them.

Apparently, Ford had just wanted to get drunk.

Madison stomped out of the bar without ordering anything. It was hard for shifters to get drunk, so Ford would be fine even if he got several more shots, but Madison was angry. He was looking for the temple, but also for Ashley. Whatever had happened to her couldn't be good, and the sooner he found her, the better it would be. He couldn't do this on his own, though, which was where Ford came in.

If he could step away from the bottle long enough.

"Where are you going?" Ford asked behind Madison.

Madison didn't look back, but he didn't need to. He could hear Ford coming after him. "I have things to do," he snapped.

"Like what? I was just taking a break."

"In a bar? I don't know about you, but I don't usually get drunk so early in the morning."

"I'm not drunk."

Ford's tone made it obvious that he found this amusing, but Madison didn't. Ford didn't understand how serious the situation was, which made Madison wonder if maybe he wasn't the guy Antonio had promised he'd find. Either that or he was a great actor, and while Madison supposed that was possible, he doubted it.

He eyed Ford over his shoulder. How could he find out if Ford was working with Antonio? He could ask questions, but he doubted Ford would answer. He had to be sneaky about it, which wasn't something he was good at.

Or he might be wrong about all of this. The only reason he suspected Antonio was involved was that he'd been reluctant to call the police and that he'd been the one to tell Madison about the note Ashley supposedly had left. There was no way that note was from her, but maybe Antonio hadn't been the one to input it into the computer.

Dammit. Madison needed to know who was involved and if he suspected Ford of being involved in something he knew nothing about. He needed to know if he could trust Ford.

"I didn't see Antonio at the hotel this morning," he said, turning to stare at Ford.

Ford cocked his head. "Who's that? One of your friends?"

It could be acting, but Madison didn't think so, which made him once again wonder who the fuck Ford was. How had he known Madison was looking for a guide if he didn't know Antonio? Who'd sent him? Or was all of this a coincidence?

It seems like too big a coincidence to be one. Besides, Ford had to know something. He wouldn't have known that Madison needed a guide if he didn't.

Madison rubbed his forehead. This was freaking confusing, and he didn't know what to do with any of the information he'd gotten since he'd met Ford. Ford knew he needed a guide, but he didn't seem to know Antonio, which pointed to the fact that he wasn't the guy Antonio had found for him. That might mean Madison was safe, but he couldn't be sure because he'd still didn't know how Ford knew that he needed a guide.

"Let's go get the supplies," Ford said, sounding entirely normal.

Madison followed him. He was confused but also a bit afraid. He was about to walk into the jungle with a guy he didn't know and whom he was pretty sure he couldn't trust. He had no idea if he'd make it out alive, but he had to believe he would and that he'd find both Ashley and the temple.

That was why he was here, and he wasn't leaving without either of those things, but depending on what Ford wanted and who he was, Madison might never leave the jungle, period.

Ford didn't know what to think of Madison. The guy was cute but a bit standoffish. He'd been asking questions that he clearly thought were sneaky, no doubt in the hope of discovering what Ford was up to. For some reason, Ford was a little sad at the thought that he would eventually betray Madison.

The guy was sweet, even when he was grumpy.

And he seemed to be grumpy most of the time. He hadn't been happy when Ford stopped to get a drink at the bar, and he was sulking as he followed Ford around. His expression made Ford want to kiss the scowl off his face, but he didn't dare move too close. He couldn't afford to like Madison. He needed to get to the temple, find out if there was anything of value there, and get the hell out as soon as he could. He wasn't sure what he'd do with Madison then, but he'd come up with something.

Abandoning someone like Madison in the middle of the jungle would get him killed, which Ford didn't want to consider. He was an asshole, and he'd be the first to admit that, but he wasn't a killer. Of course, if he left Madison in the jungle, he wouldn't kill him, but it felt too close. Ford didn't have to kill Madison himself to be responsible for his death.

"So, what do you do when you're not exploring the jungle?" he asked Madison as they poked around the store where Ford usually bought his supplies.

The owner knew him and always gave him a little extra. She liked him, and the way she treated him was the reason he always shopped here when he was in the area.

"I teach," Madison said.

He was still a little stiff, but Ford was ready to bet he'd get him to relax soon. He'd always been good with people and was at ease in large groups. He doubted the same could be said about Madison, but it was only the two of them, so he shouldn't be too uncomfortable.

"You look the job." He really did, with his glasses and neat shirts.

Madison bristled like Ford had known he would. "What does that mean?"

Ford gestured at Madison. "Well, look at you. You can't tell me you don't look like a teacher."

"Just because I have glasses?"

Ford grinned. If that was what Madison thought he was referring to, he'd go along with it. "Yeah, the glasses."

"You do realize that not everyone who wears glasses teaches, right?"

Ford couldn't stop smiling. "I'm aware. You just have the general aura of a teacher. I bet I can even guess what you teach."

"Can you?"

Ford stopped to stare at Madison. He cocked his head as he thought about what he knew about the man. It wasn't a lot, but since Madison was here to find the temple, it was probable that he was interested in history. "Are you a history teacher?"

Madison blinked. "How did you know?"

"I'm good. Now come on, prof. We have stuff to buy."

"Don't call me that."

"What should I call you, then?"

"Madison."

"I can do that. I like your name."

Madison's skin had already been flushed because of the heat, but his cheeks reddened further. It was adorable, and Ford had to look away before he did something stupid.

He was here to find the temple. He couldn't afford to start wondering what Madison's lips would feel like against his.

It wasn't the first time Ford had taken tourists into the jungle, so he knew what to get. They needed to stay light, but they'd also need food and some water. Madison seemed lost the entire time they shopped, but from the few things he picked up, it was clear it wasn't his first rodeo. That made Ford curious, but he kept his questions to himself. He didn't need to find out more about Madison. He already knew enough to be wary of how easy it would be to come to like him.

It was a relief when they were finally able to leave the shop. Ford was starting to get tense, and he could only imagine how hard it would be to spend the next few days alone in the jungle with Madison. There was no way Madison would allow him to take anything from the temple, which meant Ford would have to be sneaky. Or maybe he could find a way to get there without Madison.

He wasn't even sure the man knew where the temple was. It was entirely possible they'd spend the next week poking around in the jungle without finding anything. That wasn't something Ford was looking forward to, but at least even if that was what happened, he'd get paid. Whether or not they found the temple, Ford would still earn something from this mess, and in the end, that was all that mattered.

They went back to the car to get their backpacks ready and, from there, to the area where Ford always started his treks through the jungle. They had to leave the car behind, which was just as well. The problem was that Ford didn't know how Madison would hold up to the walking they needed to do.

"Ready?" he asked.

Madison raised his chin high. "We can go."

The sound of a car screeching to a stop nearby made them jump. Ford wasn't the only one who used this trail to get into the jungle, so it could be another guide with more tourists, but when the car doors opened, he knew that wasn't the case.

He recognized the guy from the hotel, not the one with the uniform, but the other. He was a pride member and was supposed to have talked to Diego, but Ford's brother wasn't there. He recognized another few pride members and grimaced because all of them hated him.

Just his luck.

Madison stared at the people with wide eyes. He didn't seem to see there was a problem, but Ford did, and he grabbed Madison's hand.

"What are you doing?" he asked, his voice rising.

He tried to get out of Ford's grip, and he might have managed if the pride members hadn't started shooting.

Madison screamed. He looked back at the group with wide eyes, and for a moment, Ford wondered if he was going to go down there and ask them why they were shooting. He knew why, and he wasn't about to explain. He didn't have any intention of dying, especially not here in the jungle, so he pulled Madison along.

"What's going on? Why are they shooting?" Madison asked as they ran.

"Less talking, more running," Ford told him.

"I *am* running," Madison said with a scowl just before tripping over a root and falling on his face.

Ford didn't waste time asking if he was all right. He grabbed him by the shoulders, hauled him to his feet, grabbed his hand again, and pulled him along. They needed to get away from the pride, and in the jungle, it would be fairly easy, even if the pride members shifted. Ford suspected they wouldn't, because they didn't want Madison or anyone else to realize the pride was still around, although he supposed that they wouldn't have to explain themselves if they killed Madison.

But why were they shooting? Had Diego ordered Ford and Madison killed? It hurt to think that might be the case, even though Ford had been doing everything he could to keep Diego at arm's length. Diego wanted them to be true brothers, but Ford had kept his distance because he felt he wouldn't be welcome. There was a massive difference between not being welcome and getting shot at, though. There was no way Diego would order anyone from the pride to hurt Ford. Madison, maybe, but not Ford, not when they were brothers. That meant something else was going on and that someone else was in charge of these people.

Right?

Madison was freaking out, but he supposed anyone running in the jungle while people were shooting at them would be.

His nose hurt. He'd fallen on his face, and he was grateful that Ford had picked him up. He was pretty sure he'd be dead right now if the man hadn't, but he didn't know why Ford hadn't left him behind or why these people were shooting at them.

What the fuck was happening? Were these the people who'd taken Ashley? Considering they were shooting at Madison, did that mean Ashley was dead? Madison didn't want to think about that possibility, but he wasn't sure he could avoid it.

He stumbled again, and Ford gave his arm a good shake. "You have to focus on where you're putting your feet," he growled.

"It would be easier to focus if they weren't shooting at us!"

He was pretty sure Ford rolled his eyes, even though they were running through the jungle with people fucking shooting at them. It made him want to throttle the guy, but instead, he did as Ford had asked and focused on where he was putting his feet.

He was going to die. He was sure of it.

A bullet whizzed next to his head, making him scream. It lodged in the trunk of a nearby tree, which was a relief because it would have hurt if it had lodged into Madison's skull. Ford pulled Madison to the side, and Madison went.

He had no idea where they were. This was why he needed a guide. He'd gotten lost twenty seconds after entering the jungle, and having people shooting at him wasn't helping.

"We're going to die," he moaned. "We're going to die in this fucking jungle, and no one will ever find out what happened to us."

"That's not the positive attitude I want you to have," Ford yelled back.

Madison was tempted to push him so he'd smack against one of the trees they were running past, but there was a one hundred percent chance he'd die if he ended up alone. No matter how much he disliked Ford, he needed him. That was reason enough not to trip him, even though it was tempting.

"How can I have a positive attitude when they're shooting at me?" Madison yelled.

"They're not shooting anymore."

Madison blinked. He was out of breath and sweating, and his legs and face hurt. He'd been so busy wondering how getting shot felt and if he'd die instantly that he hadn't realized that Ford was right. The people after them weren't shooting anymore. Madison could still hear them, and he was pretty sure they were coming after them, but at least they weren't trying to kill them anymore.

Not right now, anyway.

"Why were they shooting? Why did they stop?" he panted.

"Maybe we can wait until we're safe to talk about it."

Ford, the asshole, looked like he wasn't even tired. He was sweating, too, because even the most perfect man would sweat in the middle of the jungle while running from gun-crazed assholes, but he wasn't out of breath. He was running in the freaking jungle as if he were walking down the street, while Madison was next to him, huffing and puffing and stumbling over roots. It was a miracle Madison had only fallen once, and he was pretty sure his luck wouldn't hold for much longer. Knowing himself, he'd stick his foot in a hole or something, and Ford would dump his ass and abandon him to the wolves.

Or rather, to the people trying to kill him.

"I need to stop," Madison said. He was pretty sure his

lungs were going to explode if he didn't.

Ford abruptly stopped. Madison lost his balance, except this time, instead of falling face-first on the ground, he fell against Ford's chest.

His hard, sweaty chest.

Ford grabbed Madison's arms to keep him upright but didn't release him. They stood in silence, except for the sound of Madison trying to breathe and his heart attempting to escape his body through his throat.

Ford looked down. "It looks like they're not following us anymore," he murmured. "Which is a small miracle, considering how loud you are."

"I'm loud?" Madison asked, pushing away. "You're an asshole."

"Maybe so, but I'm an asshole who saved your life."

Madison tried to mop the sweat from his forehead with the back of his hand, but it was a lost cause. His cheeks burned, and he felt like a wet noodle. He wasn't one for physical activities, especially jogging. He could think of nothing worse than having to run early in the morning — or ever.

"What the fuck was that about?" he asked as he pressed his hands to his knees and tried to get his breath back.

"You tell me since you're the one they wanted to kill."

"How do you know that? Maybe they were here to kill you." Ford looked like the kind of man who knew unsavory people.

But these guys might be the ones who hurt Ashley, and they were trying to stop Madison from finding the temple.

Madison eyed Ford. Could he tell him the truth? What if he worked with those guys? He probably didn't, but how was Madison supposed to know for sure? Could he trust Ford?

He looked around. At the moment, Ford was the only person Madison had. They were alone in the jungle, and if Ford wanted to hurt Madison, it would be easy for him to do just that. Hopefully, that wasn't why he'd agreed to guide Madison. Madison had to make a decision, and he hoped it wouldn't be the wrong one.

"I'm not just here to explore the jungle," Madison explained. If Ford was working with the people who'd taken Ashley, he'd already known this. If he didn't know, he would hopefully have some tips to find the temple.

Ford arched a brow. "You don't say."

"You're an asshole."

"Maybe so, but I'm the only thing keeping you alive right now."

"I might not have gotten killed even if I were alone."

"That bullet came awfully close to your head."

Madison shuddered at the memory. It had been so close that he'd felt the air move as the bullet shot past his head. It was too easy to imagine what would have happened if the bullet had hit, and he didn't want to think about it. "I already told you I'm a teacher. I teach shifter history, and I'm looking for a temple built by a lost pride."

Ford whistled. "That would certainly explain why those people were shooting at you."

"Would it?"

"Let's walk for a bit longer," Ford said. "We'll stop soon, but I'd feel more comfortable if we put more distance between us and those guns."

Madison snorted. "As much distance as possible, please."

That made Ford smile, and for a second, Madison allowed himself to think about what it would be like to see that smile every day.

He was in trouble, and not only because people were shooting at him.

They walked for a while longer, but Ford could see Madison

was flagging. If he was honest, he wasn't far behind. He was used to traipsing around the jungle, but usually there was no one shooting at him.

Ford and Madison had barely entered the forest, and the pride had already found them. It was entirely Ford's fault. He'd used the same trail he always used when he visited the jungle, and the pride knew about it, too. It wouldn't be as easy for them to find him and Madison now that they were deeper in the jungle, though, as long as they stayed away from the trails, which they'd have to do, because the temple wasn't anywhere near a trail.

Madison had finally been honest and told Ford about the temple. They both knew what they were looking for now, so the real work could start.

Ford wanted more details, but he felt guilty. He'd told himself not to several times and that his survival was more important than some dusty ruins and whatever Madison wanted with the temple, but the professor was growing on him. Ford was starting to like him, which meant he was in trouble. Ignoring those feelings should have been easy, but nothing was ever easy in Ford's life.

Eventually, when he thought they were far enough away that the pride members wouldn't find them, he stopped. Madison was still panting, although his cheeks weren't as red anymore. He looked hopeful when Ford stopped, and when Ford gestured at him to sit on a fallen log, Madison threw himself at it as if it were a comfortable couch. Ford half expected him to hug the dead tree and maybe kiss it, but instead, Madison settled onto it and sighed in relief.

"I wasn't sure I'd be able to go on for much longer," he confessed.

"Sorry about that, but I wanted to be sure we were far enough away." Ford took his backpack off his shoulders and put it on the ground. He crouched next to it, looking for his water. His mouth felt like the Sahara Desert, and he was pretty sure Madison was in the same boat. For a few moments, neither of them spoke. They were focused on drinking water and resting, and Ford kept listening in case the pride found them. He didn't think they would, but they knew the jungle as well as he did, if not better.

The jungle was silent around them, or at least as silent as a jungle could be. Ford could hear birds and animals in the trees, and he was pretty sure something had walked past them at one point, but Madison didn't seem to notice. He was staring at his hands, and while Ford wanted to push for answers, he'd learned a long time ago that being silent got people to talk. He wasn't one who needed to fill silences, but most people were.

Madison wasn't any different.

"So, I told you I wanted to find a temple," he eventually said.

"You mentioned the lost pride."

"I'm sure you know the story, since you live here."

"They used to live in harmony with the humans until the missionaries came and ruined everything. The pride vanished into the jungle, never to be seen again."

Ford's father used to tell him the story back when Ford was a child. Ford had been fascinated, and he'd seen how proud his father was to be leading the pride from the story.

Diego was now the lost pride's alpha, and Ford was sure he was making their father proud. He, on the other hand, would have been awful as an alpha.

"That's them," Madison confirmed. "There are many stories about the lost pride and their magic, or rather, the magic of their temple and what it can do."

Ford had heard those stories, too. He'd believed them when he was a child, but growing up, he'd thought that his father was romanticizing the story and that none of it was true. He was surprised to find out that Madison seemed to believe it. "Magic isn't real."

Madison arched a brow. "Isn't it? How are you able to shift?"

Ford blinked. If Madison could tell he was a shifter, it meant Madison was one. Ford had smelled something to that effect on the other man, but they hadn't been close often, and when they had been, he'd been more interested in running for his life. "You're a shifter," he said.

Madison's jaw tightened, and he looked away. Ford didn't understand what was hard about that question, but he gave Madison time and quiet.

"I am," Madison eventually said. "Both my parents are wolf shifters, as is my sister. I'm . . . not like them, though. I rarely shift because of health issues."

Ford sucked in a breath. He couldn't imagine what life would be like if he couldn't shift whenever he felt like it. His jaguar form was part of him, something that had been there since he was born. Shifting was as natural as breathing. "What health issues?"

"I was born prematurely and have always struggled with my shift. I've been to countless doctors, and they always tell me that for their tests, I'm normal. They blame it on my difficult birth, and I'm sure they're right, but no one has ever found a way to make it easier on me."

Ford was starting to put things together. "And you think the magic of the temple will help you?"

Madison shrugged. "The temple was well known for being a healing place. People came from all over the country to pray to the gods, ask them for mercy, and be healed. There are so many stories of that happening, and even though I realize it sounds stupid, I want to find the temple. I've always been fascinated by the stories, but even more so by the people who built and protected it." He hesitated. "There are also stories about the temple bringing people back from death."

Now Ford felt like an asshole. He'd thought Madison wanted to find the temple to study it or maybe to see if he could get his hands on some artifacts, but there was so much more to it. Who did Madison want to bring back? He had to know that wouldn't be possible, right?

"Anyway, I've been coming around for a few years now," Madison continued. "I usually only work here during the summer, but I got an email from a friend. She stayed behind when I went back to work, and she sent me pictures of what I'm sure is the temple. She didn't finish the email, though, and she hasn't been answering her phone. When I got to her hotel room, the place was trashed, and the hotel manager insisted that she left a note she'd be gone for a few weeks exploring the area." Madison looked up at Ford. "She wouldn't do that. She's not here to be a tourist, and considering the email, I'm pretty sure someone hurt her. At the very least, they took her, and I'm going to find both her and the temple."

Ford swallowed. Madison sounded fierce, and Ford had no doubt he was convinced of what he was saying, but it wouldn't be as easy as saying the words. He was right about the temple. It had always been a secret place, and the pride wouldn't let him go anywhere near it, even if his reasons for wanting to find it were good. Ford should tell Madison all of that, but he wasn't sure he could.

He needed this money. He needed Madison to see this through, find the temple, and hopefully, find something valuable inside of it. Neither Madison nor Diego would ever forgive Ford if he stole something there, but at the moment, Ford didn't care.

Diego had sent his people to shoot at him and possibly kill him. He always told Ford he wanted them to be real siblings, to be close, but Ford didn't quite believe him.

"So you're not planning on going back?" he asked

Madison.

The man looked at him like he was nuts. "What haven't you understood of what I said? I'll find both my friend and the temple. By the time I'm done, I'll finally be able to shift."

Ford hoped for his sake that everything he was saying would eventually come true, but he had doubts. Life never went that way.

CHAPTER SIX

Madison hadn't planned to tell Ford all of that, but he was terrified and exhausted and needed a friend. He needed someone to be there for him, and since he and Ford were alone in the jungle, there was only one person who could do that.

The problem was that all of this felt like a setup. How had those people found them so easily? Had Ford told them where he and Madison would enter the jungle? But he'd risked his life, too. He could have been shot instead of Madison, so maybe it was a coincidence.

"Well, I hope you'll get everything you want," Ford said as he got to his feet. "I'll help you find the temple."

Madison was still convinced of what he wanted to do. He wanted to find the temple and, even more so, Ashley. He was scared, though, and as he rose from the dead tree, he looked around. "I'm not changing my mind, but maybe we should head back for now. We need to regroup and hire more people." As it was, it would be way too easy for those guys to kill both Madison and Ford. Madison might want to find the temple, but he wasn't an idiot. It wouldn't do him any good if he was dead or died shortly after.

Ford cocked his head. "You were just saying that you wanted to find the temple."

"I do, but it won't do me any good if I'm dead."

"I won't let them hurt you."

"How are you going to stop the bullets?"

"They stopped shooting."

"Because we ran away. We need more people and

protection." Madison had never felt afraid to be in the jungle on his own. Well, he'd never actually been on his own. He usually came here with a group of people, including Ashley. They had each other's back, but then they'd never needed to worry about anything more than wild animals.

This situation was completely different, and Madison needed to be reassured. He had to know he'd be all right by the end of this, and he didn't trust Ford to protect him.

"I'm not taking you back after all of this," Ford said.

Madison looked at him in shock. "You're my guide. I'm paying you to do what I asked."

"You're paying me to find your temple, and that's what I'll do. Going back would waste time. Besides, they might be waiting for us."

"Then we go another way. You have to see this is stupid."

Ford folded his arms over his chest. "What I see is that you're afraid."

Madison was. He was terrified that he was going to die, and there was nothing wrong with that, but for some reason, he felt belittled by Ford's words. He shouldn't be afraid. He was a wolf shifter, and he should face danger head-on like Ford was suggesting. His mother would tell him to raise his chin and move on and that he shouldn't show anyone his weaknesses.

Ford already knew one of Madison's weaknesses.

"Come on," Ford said soothingly. "I'll protect you."

But Madison couldn't trust him. He grabbed his backpack and turned in the direction from which they'd come, hoping the shooters were gone. Surely, they weren't hiding behind the trees waiting for him. They'd stopped shooting, which meant they weren't anywhere close by.

Or at least, that was what Madison was trying to convince himself of.

He started walking. He couldn't hear Ford coming after

him, so it looked like the guy wasn't going to help him find his way out of the jungle. If he thought Madison was going to pay him after that, he had another think coming. Madison could find his way out of the jungle on his own.

Hopefully.

It took almost no time for him not to be able to see Ford again. Just a few steps, and when Madison turned around, he could only see trees. It scared him, but it also pushed him forward.

He wasn't weak. He might be small and relatively weak, but he'd been coming here for a few years now. He knew this jungle.

He turned around to start walking again and found himself face-to-face with a gigantic snake. They stared each other in the eyes, and Madison's body started to tremble. He opened his mouth, and the scream came out before he could stop himself.

He stumbled back, and his foot caught on a root. His world tilted, and he hit the ground hard. He scrambled back, the snake still staring at him, as something came crashing toward him between the trees. Was it another wild animal? Were they going to eat him?

Ford burst from between the trees. His eyes were wide as he looked around, a machete raised high as if to defend Madison. For a moment, neither of them moved.

Then, the snake slithered closer, and Madison started freaking out again.

"What's going on?" Ford asked.

"*What's going on?* Can't you see the snake?"

"Well, I can see it, but I'm not sure why you were screaming. Did you see someone?"

"This snake is going to eat me."

Ford stared. "You screamed because of the snake?"

"Why else would I scream?"

Ford rolled his eyes and put away his machete. He came closer, and Madison watched with wide eyes as he pushed the snake away with a foot. The snake didn't seem bothered, even though it was as big as Ford's leg. It allowed Ford to guide him away, and Madison quickly got to his feet. He needed to get as far as possible from the snake, even if the thing wasn't to eat him.

"Wait," Ford said as he rushed to keep up with Madison. "Where are you going?"

"I already told you."

"So you're abandoning your friend?"

That was enough to make Madison stop. He turned and glared at Ford, fighting the impulse to strangle him. "I'm not."

"But you're leaving."

"Only temporarily."

"I understand why you want to, but think about it. If the people who shot at us are the ones who got your friend, they know we're here. They also probably know we're looking for the temple. Are you willing to risk them finding it before you?"

Madison narrowed his eyes. "I know what you're doing."

"I'm not doing anything but telling you the truth. I understand why you're afraid, but you don't have to be. I'll protect you."

Madison wanted to believe that. He wanted to believe that by the time this was over, he'd still be in one piece and breathing.

He had a choice to make. He could either go back and allow fear to guide his steps or push on and trust Ford to protect him.

He wasn't a coward. Not being able to shift didn't mean he was weak.

So he raised his chin. "Show me the way, then. Let's find

the temple." And Ashley.

Madison was adorable. Ford was pretty sure the professor would kick his ass if he as much as mentioned that, though, so he pressed his lips together and led Madison back to the fallen tree where they'd sat earlier.

It was good Ford had managed to change Madison's mind. They needed to get to the temple, and fast. Diego knew they were here, which meant he'd sent the pride to stop them. Ford wasn't looking forward to facing his brother in this situation, so it would be best for him and Madison to get to the temple, grab whatever they could, and get out.

Except that wasn't Madison's plan.

Madison wasn't here to grab things from the temple. He was here to heal, help his friend, and probably take enough pictures to fill an entire memory card. Ford felt like an ass-hole, but he was a survivor. He needed to do what was best for himself, not for Diego or Madison.

"I have conditions when it comes to paying you," Madison said.

He was going in the general direction in which Ford thought the temple was, so he followed. "What conditions? I'm your guide. I brought you to the jungle, and I'll guide you through it."

Madison ignored him. "You can't be an asshole. You can't mention anything about me not being able to shift."

Ford had to try hard not to smile. "I can do that."

Madison looked at him suspiciously. "I'm not sure you can, but I guess we'll find out. I also want you to stop smiling like that," he added, gesturing at Ford's face.

Ford couldn't restrain himself anymore. He couldn't fight a losing battle, so he grinned. "I wasn't smiling."

"Well, you are now, and it's annoying."

"Unfortunately, that's the face I was born with, so you're going to have to find a way to deal with it," Ford said happily. "Now, about this temple. What do you know about it?"

Ford remembered the old stories and had a vague idea of where the temple was located. He'd never been allowed there, not even as a child, but he lived with the pride long enough to know their traditions and that they'd protect the temple with their lives. It was the only thing left from the lost pride that had retreated into the jungle and was still sacred.

Ford told himself not to feel guilty. It was just a few bits of stone stacked together, and that was that. No matter what people believed, Ford doubted there was magic in it, and even less so, gods. If gods did exist, they had better things to do than to hang around a ruined temple in the jungle.

"I don't know much," Madison said as he dug into his pocket and took out a piece of paper. "I've been looking through Ashley's things and found this map."

Ford took it. He wasn't surprised to see it was a map of the area. Ashley had been working methodically, exploring parts of the jungle and crossing them out once she was sure the temple wasn't there. She'd been getting closer, leaving only one area not crossed out. It was vast but not big enough not to be able to find the temple if one knew what to look for.

"I can take you there," Ford said.

"That's what I'm paying you for."

"We better start walking, then."

It wouldn't be a short walk. The temple had been built deep in the jungle for a reason. Only the pride and the people they thought deserved it saw the temple, and no one was supposed to stumble onto the place by mistake. It would take days to get there, and that wasn't considering the pride hunting them. They wouldn't let Ford and Madison get there without attempting to stop them. Ford wasn't looking forward to finding out how they'd do that.

So he started walking. Madison kept up surprisingly well now that he wasn't running for his life. He bitched and complained about pretty much everything, but Ford had expected that. It was actually nice to listen to Madison's voice. It drowned out the sounds of the jungle that Ford was so used to, and it made him feel less alone.

Madison wasn't going anywhere until he found the temple, and while Ford hoped it wouldn't take them more than a few days, he didn't count on that. They had to dodge the pride's attacks, get to the temple, and get inside. It wasn't going to be easy.

But for now, things *were* easy. They walked for hours, stopping a few times to eat and drink. Even Madison's complaining started to fade after a while, maybe because he was too tired to speak. The silence was peaceful, and Ford basked in it for as long as he could. Eventually, the night started falling, and Ford knew they couldn't continue.

They were shifters, even though Madison had a hard time with it. They would have been okay to continue walking if they hadn't been so tired, but Ford wasn't willing to risk it. He was exhausted, and there was no way Madison wasn't. They needed a good night's sleep, or at the very least, a good chunk of time to rest.

He paused and looked around. He didn't usually go so deep when he had tourists with him, so he didn't have the same opportunities as he usually did. He didn't recognize the area and didn't know where they could find a safe spot to rest and spend the night.

The middle of the jungle would have to do.

He found another fallen tree, decided this place was as good as any, and dropped his backpack next to it. "We'll stop for the night,"

"Are you sure we should? What if they find us?" Madison asked, nervously looking behind himself.

"If they haven't found us by following the sound of your voice, I doubt they will."

Madison glared. "I don't speak that much."

"I'm sorry to say I disagree. You talk more than my neighbor, and she's a chatterbox." The world might end if Mrs. Garcia and Madison ever met.

Madison stomped closer and dropped his backpack. "I don't like you," he declared.

Ford grinned. "That's a pity, because I like you." He wiggled his eyebrows. "Even though you're not here for sex."

Madison's cheeks flushed. It was beautiful to see, and Ford was tempted to lean closer and kiss him. He was pretty sure that if he did that, Madison would punch him, which wasn't something he wanted to happen. So he kept his lips to himself and looked around.

"I'm going to shift and hunt something to eat," he told Madison.

"You don't have to do that."

"Maybe not, but I don't know about you, but a nice hot meal would be great. Can you get a fire going?"

"Probably."

"Let me rephrase that. Can you get a fire going without burning down the entire jungle?"

Madison's glare was back. "Go hunt. I'll take care of everything here."

Ford wasn't sure he could trust Madison, but he didn't have a choice. He winked, then started shedding his clothes. Madison made a strangled noise and turned around, crouched next to his backpack, and made himself busy taking things out of it. Ford went as slowly as he could because he enjoyed flustering Madison. Eventually, he was entirely naked, and since he didn't fancy getting mosquito bites on his dick, he quickly shifted.

The world around him changed. His vision was different

when he was in his jaguar form, but no less beautiful. In this form, he felt that he belonged in the jungle. It was welcoming him, and he stretched, enjoying the feeling.

He could feel Madison's gaze on him, but he didn't turn again. They each had their task, and Ford needed to get moving if they wanted to eat tonight.

But first, he turned to Madison. The other man was staring at him, and even though he quickly looked away when Ford faced him, Ford had noticed. It made him grin, which he'd been told was terrifying when he was in this form, but he didn't think Madison was afraid of him.

No, clearly what Madison felt was miles away from fear, mirroring how Ford felt about him.

This could only end in a disaster, but that was Ford's entire life.

Ford was beautiful. He was gorgeous in both his forms, but something in his jaguar form made Madison want to pet him. He tried to remember if jaguars purred, but he didn't know.

And he wasn't going to find out.

He looked down at what he was doing, and by the time he glanced up again, Ford was gone. That was just as well, because Madison was starving and ready to sleep for a solid twelve hours. He doubted he'd have the opportunity to do that, but he could at least eat.

Which meant lighting a fire. It wouldn't be the first time Madison had done that, but it always took him a while, especially given how humid the jungle was. He wanted to have the fire going by the time Ford came back, so he got to work.

He hadn't been surprised to see Ford's animal form. He'd suspected the man could shift into some kind of big cat. It was in his eyes and even more so in how he moved as a human. Even as he ran for his life, he was graceful and fast. The jaguar shone through his human skin, and the ease in which Ford had shifted made Madison jealous.

He had to get over that. There was no changing the way he was, and he didn't *want* to change. He was perfectly fine the way he was, as his grandmother had always said. Madison was here to find the temple for her, and even though he didn't believe in gods, he'd pray. He had no idea how the magic worked and how it could bring people back from death, but he was ready to try anything to get his grandma back. She was one of two people who truly cared about him, and her death had left a crater in his life.

He'd spent long years feeling like he was watching his family from the outside and wishing they would care about him the way they cared about each other. Thirty-eight years of feeling like that was an eternity. He didn't care that they felt he wasn't enough anymore. He didn't need them. He needed his sister and his grandmother, and that was it.

The fire was going by the time Ford came back. Madison made sure not to look at him because he didn't fancy staring his dinner in the eyes. He didn't even care what animal it was. He'd be fine if he couldn't see its face.

Besides, Ford didn't ask for any help with cleaning dinner. He took care of all of that himself, even the cooking, and Madison was begrudgingly impressed. He made sure not to say anything about it, not even when they started eating. Ford was smug enough as it was, and Madison didn't need to make his ego even bigger.

Even though dinner was delicious.

It was clear Ford was used to spending time in the jungle, but then, he was a guide. He knew what he was doing and had thought of bringing along spices and salt. It was tasty enough not to make Madison think of the food back home, and by the time he was done eating, he felt ready to sleep.

"Go to bed," Ford told him. "I'll clean up and take care of

the fire."

He wouldn't have to ask twice. Madison stretched out on the pad he'd brought, closed his eyes, and told his body it was time for rest. The problem was that back at home, Madison slept with earplugs on, a facemask, and a white noise machine, because he was such a light sleeper that any noise woke him up. He was used to falling asleep with the sound of the ocean in his ears, but there was nothing like that here. He always had a hard time sleeping when he came to the jungle, and even though he was exhausted, this time wasn't any different.

There were too many strange noises. The forest had come alive at night, and branches cracked around Madison. He could hear animals moving, calling to each other, and possibly plotting to eat him. Was he going to wake up to a bird nibbling on his toes?

"You're safe," Ford whispered. "I'll keep an eye on you during the night. No one is going to hurt you while you sleep, Madison."

Madison was dismayed that Ford was able to read him so well, although not surprised. He'd always been one to broadcast his feelings, good or bad.

"I'm fine," he said in a harsh voice.

"I'm sure you are, but you need rest. I'm going to shift again, all right?"

"You need rest, too."

"And I'll get it. I'm used to this, remember? I'm a professional guide. You should listen to me."

It probably was a bad idea, but Madison decided to do just that.

He closed his eyes and told himself to go to sleep again. He didn't know if he could trust Ford, but he supposed he'd find out when he woke up.

CHAPTER SEVEN

Madison was struggling. He kept telling himself to put one foot in front of the other and continue walking, but his entire body ached, and his legs felt like lead. Even when he came to the jungle over the summer, he never walked as much as he was walking now. It was good he hadn't brought his smartwatch, because it would have stopped working in protest.

He felt like a different person. None of this was like him. He was the kind of person who stayed in his office and had others do the hard work. He poked around the jungle for a few months every year, but that was it. The rest of the time, he was very much a couch potato, and he'd started missing his couch about ten minutes after climbing out of the plane. He wanted to go home.

But he wanted to see his grandmother again even more.

Things were oddly tense with Ford. Madison still had no idea what to think of the guy, and they'd been walking in silence most of the morning. They'd woken up early, and when Madison had opened his eyes, he'd found Ford already in his human form and fully dressed. The man had been making instant coffee on the fire and cheerfully offered Madison a cup. Madison stared at him for a moment, unable to comprehend what he saw.

How could anyone be that cheerful so early in the morning, especially after being chased, shot at, and walking the entire day before? Madison's brain wasn't even fully online yet, and they'd already been walking for an hour.

Well, Ford was walking. Madison was dragging his feet and couldn't see that changing anytime soon. He wanted to find Ashley and the temple but wasn't sure his body would keep up with the program.

He supposed he could ask Ford to slow down. Ford would, if anything because he wanted to be paid. But Madison didn't want to appear weak. He'd already told Ford about his shifting problems and everything else. He hadn't told him the entire truth about what he hoped to find in the temple, but Ford didn't need to know about Madison's grandmother and what Madison was planning on doing if the legends about the temple were right.

Most of the people Madison worked with didn't have the same hope that the temple's magic was real, and he didn't want to make enemies out of them or have them make fun of him. It was a secret he'd kept to himself. Hopefully, he wouldn't have a reason to do so for much longer. Once they found the temple and he managed to find out how to make the magic work, Madison would get his grandmother back, and he could show everyone — including his mother — that he wasn't a nutty professor.

He stumbled for what had to be the hundredth time today. He was pretty sure his toes were going to be bruised by the time the day was over, but that was just a small ache to add to the long list of pains he already felt everywhere else in his body. Thankfully, he managed to catch himself on a tree and paused for a few seconds, the time to get his breath back.

"Everything okay?" Ford asked, stopping to look at Madison.

"I'm fine." Madison's tone was brusque, but he couldn't find it in himself to be nice, especially not to Ford. He wanted to fuck the man as much as he wanted to strangle him, which wasn't something he usually felt. His emotions had never been strong, at least when it came to sex and relationships.

He'd had both, but he hadn't been sad when they'd ended.

He wouldn't be sad when Ford returned to his life, and Madison went home. He didn't have a reason to feel that way, after all.

Ford stared at him for a moment before nodding. "Well, we should continue walking."

So that was what they did. Madison stumbled about a dozen more times, and he could feel himself reaching the end of his patience. He started grumbling and praying they were about to stop, even though they couldn't afford to waste time.

"You're noisy again," Ford said without turning.

"I'm not noisy. If you want me to be, though, I can do that." He opened his mouth to yell, but the snap of a branch behind him made him freeze. He had no idea what was coming after him, but from the sound of it, it was big, and it was running.

"Shit," Ford said as he grabbed Madison's arm.

Madison just had the time to see something black streak toward them. Ford was pulling on his arm, and he rushed to follow the silent order. He didn't want to be dinner to whatever creature was coming.

"Run!" Ford ordered.

"What do you think I'm doing?"

"Not running fast enough!"

That was probably true. Madison was afraid to look back but could hear the animal coming after them. Hell, was it even an animal, or was it a shifter? There was no way for him to know unless he sniffed it, and he wasn't about to stop and ask if he could. Besides, did it matter? Whether this was a real animal or a shifter, they were planning on hurting him, which wasn't something he was looking forward to.

"You should shift!" he yelled at Ford because it felt useless to continue running. Madison would never be able to shift fast enough to do something about that, but Ford could.

"I might if there was only one of them."

Madison stumbled again. "What do you mean?"

Ford held him up and pulled him forward. "It isn't just one jaguar. It's a group, and I can't fight all of them. We need to escape."

Madison was on board with that. He went faster, feeling better at the thought that Ford would help him up if he fell. He hadn't been lying when he'd said he'd protect Madison, even though Madison didn't understand why. It couldn't be because he was paying him, right? Surely if Ford had to choose between being eaten by a jaguar and getting paid by Madison, he wouldn't hesitate. Madison was slowing him down, but he didn't seem ready to leave him behind. It gave Madison hope that they'd both eventually make it out of the jungle.

But that hope could still be dashed, so he pushed himself even harder. They needed to get away from whatever was coming after them, and they needed to do it now.

It was the pride. Ford hadn't been close enough to figure out if the jaguars running after him and Madison were shifters or animals, but the answer was obvious anyway. There was only one reason for a group of jaguars to come after two people.

They were shifters, and they were angry.

Jaguars were usually loners, yet these were attacking in a group. That was what made them dangerous and the reason Ford couldn't fight back. There were too many of them, and if he tried to fight, he'd end up dead. It wasn't something he wanted to contemplate, which was why he and Madison were running.

"I hate this," Madison grumbled as he ran.

His ability to bitch even while he was running was astounding, but as long as he was going fast, Ford didn't care what he was saying. The problem was that they were too slow. The jaguars had four paws and knew the jungle like the back of their hands. They'd catch up to Madison and Ford soon, and they'd be in trouble when it happened.

They were already in trouble. Madison wasn't fast to begin with, and he was slowing down with every step he took. Ford couldn't fight back because there were too many jaguars, so he'd be shredded to pieces even if he shifted.

As if they weren't already in enough trouble, their problems multiplied when Ford heard the sound of water moving.

He looked back, not surprised to see the jaguars were still following. They darted around the trees, never slowing down, and it felt like they were playing with their prey. They probably were. They could have caught Ford and Madison easily, but they were still making them run.

The one in front snarled and exposed his teeth. Ford narrowed his eyes and flipped him the bird. They shared the same coloring but weren't family, and he'd kick that jaguar's ass if he had the chance.

"There's a river in front of us," Madison panted.

"I can hear it."

"We're stuck. We're going to die, and they're going to eat us, and no one will ever know what happened to us."

He sounded resigned and freaked out at the same time, which was a feat, but Ford wasn't done fighting. He wasn't dying here, dammit. At the moment, he didn't even care about the temple or artifacts and money. He just cared about making it out alive, and he would, no matter the cost.

He ran faster, ignoring Madison's squeak as he pulled him along. They needed to lose the jaguars for a moment, just enough time to throw Madison into the river and allow him to swim to the other side.

Ford thought they were safe when he saw a bridge, only to realize that it had broken a long time ago and that part of it was dangling into the river.

"Dammit," he said as he pushed Madison forward. "You need to swim to the other side. I'll stay back and keep an eye on them. I'll fight them if they try to go after you, but I can't promise I'll win."

Madison turned wide eyes toward him. "I can't swim."

"What?" Ford stared. "How can you not swim? Everyone can swim."

"Everyone except me, apparently. I couldn't go in the water when I was a kid because I had a lot of ear infections."

Ford dismissed him. He turned to face the first jaguar, who he could hear crashing through the trees. "I'm going to shift, but I don't know how long I'll be able to keep them at bay. I'm sorry, Madison." Considering how hard Madison had told him it was for him to shift, Ford doubted he'd get far, even if he turned into a wolf. Ford would try to protect him, but he was only one man.

He dropped his backpack and started shifting. He didn't waste time taking off his clothes, thankful he'd trained to get out of them while he was in his jaguar form. It enabled him to be ready when the first jaguar appeared, even though he was still wearing his underwear.

"We have to find another way," Madison said.

But Ford couldn't answer. The first jaguar crashed through the bushes, appearing in front of them. He licked his lips, and Ford narrowed his eyes.

They weren't friends or family. They weren't even part of the same pride. Ford was a loner, and this was one of the reasons he was. Diego had been nice and had said all the right things, but in the end, he'd been lying. He'd sent his people after Ford and had ordered them to shoot at him and Madison and possibly kill them. Ford had been right not to trust him, even though it hurt to admit it.

It would hurt even more to fight the jaguar.

The other shifter yowled and threw himself at Ford. Ford

heard Madison squeak, but he couldn't focus on him. He had to fight back if he didn't want to die right away. He prepared himself to do just that.

As soon as the jaguar collided with him, Ford brought up his back paws. He went backward, landing on his back with the other jaguar on top of him. His paws were between them, though, and he used them to push the other jaguar away as he dug his claws into the jaguar's stomach. The jaguar yowled again and sprang away, and for a moment, they stared at each other. Blood dripped to the ground under the jaguar's stomach, but the fight wasn't over.

It wouldn't be until Ford was dead.

They moved forward again, clashing in a flurry of claws and fangs. Ford hissed when a claw caught him in the shoulder, but he couldn't focus on the pain. He didn't want Madison to have to watch him die and, worse, to experience the pain of claws tearing through him. The professor had grown on him, even though Ford didn't understand why.

Ford wasn't stupid enough to think the jaguars would let Madison go once he died. He hoped to give Madison a chance and more time. He wasn't sure what Madison could do on his own, but hopefully, he wasn't as clumsy as Ford thought.

A scream startled Ford, and when he and the jaguar moved apart, he frantically looked around to find Madison. His eyes widened at the sight of the professor swinging over the river, screaming his head off.

What the fuck was he doing? How was this better than swimming or at least attempting to swim?

Madison swung through the air, and thankfully, whatever he was swinging from didn't break. Ford held his breath, thinking that Madison wouldn't make it. It looked like he wouldn't let go of the rope, which meant he'd swing right back to the wrong side of the river.

But Madison let go. He flew into the jungle, disappearing

from sight. Ford heard a crash, then a yell, and he wondered if Madison had gotten hurt. The rope was swinging back, but Ford doubted he'd be able to use it without Madison's weight on it.

He was still going to try.

He quickly shifted, grabbed his backpack, and rushed toward the rope. The jaguar crashed behind him, growling and snarling. Madison hooked his backpack over his shoulders and launched himself toward the rope.

For a moment, he was airborne. It was terrifying but also exhilarating. If they were lucky, they'd manage to get out of this mess, which was all Ford wanted. He hadn't expected Madison to do something like this, and he was really fucking proud.

His fingertips brushed against the rope, and he snatched it up. It jarred his wounded shoulder, but he gritted his teeth and went along with the movement, swinging over the river. It wasn't enough to get him to the other side, and he had to drop into the river.

The water was cold and a shock to his system. He pushed the fear and pain away and quickly swam until he reached the safe side of the river. He didn't know where Madison had ended up, but the first thing he needed to do was to get out of the water. Then, he could look for him.

"Let me help you," a voice said, grabbing his hand as he climbed out.

Ford's heart stuttered, and he looked up into Madison's eyes. "You made it."

Madison grinned. "Did you really think I was going to allow them to keep me from the temple?"

Ford laughed, then shivered. "I suppose I should have known you wouldn't. Come on. We need to continue running."

Madison nodded and pulled Ford forward. Their roles

were reversed, but it didn't feel wrong. Madison had followed him until now, and it was Ford's turn to follow. It was odd and not something Ford was used to, but he was starting to realize that Madison was like no one he'd ever known.

And that was scarier than facing a pissed-off jaguar.

Madison was freaking out, even though he was trying to appear strong. He didn't want Ford to think he was weak and unable to deal with what was happening, even though that was what he felt like.

His hands still shook. He couldn't believe what he'd done, but he'd been desperate, and when he saw a rope hanging from a tree, he knew what he had to do. He might not be able to swim, but he'd spent a lot of his childhood climbing trees, and he remembered how that worked. It hadn't been as easy as when he was a kid, but he'd carried the rope up the tree, had checked that it was securely tied around one of the thickest branches, and then he'd swung.

He was pretty sure the entire jungle had heard him scream, but he didn't care. He made it out in one piece, a bit more bruised than before but alive. His ass hurt from the landing, and he'd almost slammed face-first into a tree, but he and Ford were on the other side of the river and were running again. Hopefully, this would give them enough time to escape the jaguars, but they'd have to stop soon. Ford was still wet, and it couldn't be comfortable.

"You should shift," he panted.

"Only if you do, too."

Madison almost rolled his eyes. "It would take too much time, and we can't afford to waste the advantage we have. You'll be faster if you shift."

"You think I'm going to leave you behind?"

Madison wouldn't have been surprised if Ford had done

just that. He was here to guide Madison, not to sacrifice himself fighting a bunch of jaguars. Madison didn't want anyone to get hurt for him, and Ford had risked a lot by staying behind.

Madison couldn't help but wonder who the jaguars were. Ford was a jaguar shifter, after all. Were they part of the same pride? But if they were, why had they attacked Ford? Maybe they were here for him and not Madison, although Madison had a hard time believing that. If these jaguars had been shifters—and he believed they were—they were probably trying to protect the temple and its magic. Killing anyone who tried to find it didn't seem like the best idea, but what did Madison know?

But where did Ford stand if the jaguars were shifters trying to protect the temple? He hadn't hesitated to fight back, so maybe he wasn't a pride member. Madison knew enough to be aware of the fact that jaguars were loners. They didn't often live in groups, unlike wolves. Maybe that was what Ford was. Maybe he was a loner and stayed away from the local pride, and they weren't happy that he was showing a human where their temple was.

The implications were incredible. If that was what was happening, it meant the lost pride wasn't lost, or at least not entirely. The individuals wouldn't be the same, of course, but they were still doing what the original pride had done, which was protecting their territory and the temple.

They couldn't know that Madison wasn't human and only wanted the magic the temple wielded to help him, but maybe they'd be coming after him even if they did. They weren't exactly friendly, and while it could be a coincidence, Madison doubted he had two different groups coming after him. The jaguars were probably the same guys who'd been shooting at him and Ford, which meant they wanted him dead.

So much for the pride welcoming the people who needed

their magic. They had in the past, but clearly, not anymore.

Madison's foot hit something, and he fell forward. Like always, Ford was there for him, grabbing his arm and pulling him close. For a moment, Madison pressed against his body. He smelled blood and jerked back, but he didn't have time to say anything or even to check where Ford was wounded. Ford grabbed his hand and pulled him forward, running even faster now.

"Less tripping and more running," he ordered.

He was right. Whatever was happening, no matter how many questions Madison had, the first thing they needed to do was to be safe. That meant ditching the jaguars, which in turn meant running harder than he ever had.

Even if the jaguars didn't kill him, he might just die anyway.

Chapter Eight

Ford didn't know how long they ran. He never slowed down, pulling Madison along when he started flagging. Ford was exhausted, too, but they needed to get as far away from the jaguars as possible.

It was the worst time of his life. He was wet, and he couldn't get dry because of the humidity in the air. The only item of clothing he hadn't ditched earlier were his boxer briefs, which clung to his groin while exposing the rest of his body to mosquitoes and other insects. He was barefoot, which didn't make running through the jungle easy. He was thankful he hadn't cut himself on anything yet, but it was bound to happen, which meant he'd need to stop soon. He had more clothes and another pair of shoes in his backpack, but he needed time to put them on.

"I can't hear them anymore," Madison said.

He sounded breathless, and Ford wondered if he was about to break. Ford felt like he might and could only imagine how Madison felt. Ford had the adrenaline of the fight to sustain him to run, but not Madison.

He'd been fucking brave, and Ford was impressed. It would have been easy for Madison to give up and wait around until Ford was done fighting, but he hadn't. He'd found a solution and a way to reach the other side of the river, and they'd made it out alive. They still had a chance to find the temple.

As long as they stopped soon, anyway.

Ford slowed down, turning to peer at the jungle. There

were trees everywhere, making running hard, but it also concealed their path. He held his breath and listened, but like Madison had said, he couldn't hear anything. It looked like they were alone, and while he stayed tense for a second, he eventually dropped his backpack and slumped against a tree.

Soft hands touching his shoulder made him jerk back. He opened his eyes to find Madison standing in front of him, both of his hands raised as if he thought Ford believed he was a danger.

"You're wounded," Madison said.

"Just a scratch." A scratch that hurt like hell, but Ford would survive.

"You could get an infection from the water or the jaguar's claws. We need to clean it."

"I have stuff in my backpack."

"Me, too." Madison was serious as he crouched next to their backpacks and started rooting through his.

Ford was exhausted. He wanted nothing more than to drop on his ass and rest for a week, but instead, he leaned down to open his bag. It was a little damp on the outside, but waterproof, so everything had made it through, including the shoes at the bottom of the bag. By the time Madison had taken out everything he needed to take care of Ford's shoulder, Ford was once again wearing pants and shoes. He'd ditched his boxers, and Madison hadn't even blushed. He'd been too busy, which had made Ford smile. The man was adorable, but he could also be incredibly focused.

"Those weren't animals," Madison murmured as he started cleaning the wound on Ford's shoulder.

Ford swallowed. "I don't think they were, no."

"They were the same people who shot at us."

"Probably." Ford should tell him the truth, but how could he?

He didn't know what to do. He couldn't afford to further

alienate his brother and the pride. Madison would eventually go home, but Ford lived here. If he made an enemy of the pride, he'd die or be forced to run, and he didn't want to start from scratch again.

He wasn't sure how to get out of this situation. The first step should be to call Diego, but the betrayal tasted sour on Ford's tongue. He couldn't believe his brother was doing this, but he should. Diego was an alpha, and he'd always made it clear that the pride was important to him.

Ford had a choice to make. He could either say fuck it and take Madison to the temple or betray Madison and hand him over to the pride. Ford's heart hurt at the thought of doing that, but maybe the pride wouldn't hurt Madison if he did. They could send him home, and everyone would be happy.

Except for Madison, who was here because he had such a hard time shifting.

He was taking care of Ford as if he cared about him. After cleaning the wound, he wrapped it up and ordered Ford to tell him if it felt painful or warm to the touch. He was worried that Ford would get an infection, and it touched Ford in a way few things had. Only his father had ever cared for him like that. Even his mother hadn't, thinking about herself more than she'd ever thought about him. The fact that Madison, a man Ford barely knew, was taking care of him made Ford's eyes prickle with tears.

But he couldn't cry. He had to find a way out of this mess, and crying wouldn't help.

Eventually, Madison sat down and leaned against a tree facing Ford. For a moment, they were silent, with the only sounds coming from the forest and their heavy breathing.

"What's it like to shift so effortlessly?" Madison asked in a whisper.

He had to have asked other people that before, but now, he was asking Ford.

"It's natural, like breathing. It doesn't feel any different than being human. It's what we were made to be and do."

"I can see that."

Except he couldn't. He'd told Ford that shifting was tortuous for him, and it sounded like he'd never found any pleasure in doing so. He'd been made to be both a human and a wolf. Yet it was easier for him to stay human, and that wasn't right. It wasn't *fair*, but life never was.

And that was why they were in this situation and why Ford had to make an impossible decision.

Eventually, they got to their feet and started walking again. They couldn't afford to stay back in case the jaguars found them, and the conversation had gotten a bit heavy for Madison's taste. He didn't want to talk about what normal shifting was like. He'd been told time and time again, and every time, it hurt like hell. He wanted to shift and feel like it was natural the way Ford had described, but it would never be like that for him. He'd thought he'd made his peace with it, but maybe not.

It was hard to think straight. Madison had never been in a situation where he had to run for his life like he was now, and his brain couldn't catch up. The fact that they were in a freaking jungle and it was so hot and humid didn't help, and neither did the insects and mosquitoes. By the time Ford finally allowed them to stop for the night, Madison's entire body was itching, and his glasses kept slipping down his nose because he was sweating so much. He wanted nothing more than to throw himself in a shower, but they were so far away from civilization that Madison couldn't help but wonder if he'd ever see a bed again.

He almost kissed Ford when the man decided they needed to stop. He managed to resist the urge, instead focusing on what was still left to do before he could go to bed. He was hungry, but he didn't want Ford to go hunting tonight, so he told him that.

"I can shift," Ford insisted. "It's just a scratch."

"You don't need to shift. We have enough protein bars and other stuff to last us for a few days. Besides, you need your strength in case they attack us again."

Madison thought that it would be better for Ford to leave. These people were after Madison, and he felt horrible at the thought of putting anyone else in danger. Unfortunately, he'd be utterly lost if Ford were to dump him in the jungle, but he didn't want to consider that. He could do this on his own. He should try to convince Ford to go back.

He chewed on his lower lip as he stared at the fire. Ford needed the money, but he needed his life more. Madison wasn't rich, but he could afford to pay Ford. He didn't want to be left alone, but maybe it was time to face the fact that it would be safer for Ford.

"I'll pay you even if you want to go back now," he said.

Ford had been chewing on a protein bar but quickly swallowed and stared at Madison. His shirt was open, and Madison could see a peek of the bandages he'd put on Ford's shoulder. He'd checked the wound again after they'd stopped, relieved to see it wasn't bleeding anymore. The most dangerous thing now was an infection. That was pretty much the worst thing that could happen, considering where they were.

"Are you telling me to dump you?" Ford asked.

"I can find my way to the temple on my own. I've been exploring this jungle for a few years now."

"Yet you needed a guide."

"Only because it's easier. You know the jungle better than I do, but that doesn't mean I don't know it at all."

"Did you know the rope was there?"

Madison shook his head. "I had no idea and don't know

who left it there." And he didn't care.

He'd been frantic, looking for a way to save himself. He wanted to help Ford, but how? He couldn't take on a jaguar in his human form, and Ford had been fighting to give him time to run. He'd hoped that Ford would be able to disengage once he realized Madison wasn't there anymore, and that had meant finding a way to cross the river.

That was when Madison had seen the rope. He'd wondered if someone else had used it to cross the river, but he'd probably never find out, and honestly, he didn't care much. The rope had saved him and Ford, and *that* was what he cared about.

"Look, they're after me," he told Ford. "They're not going to stop until they get me, and I can't let you get hurt."

"I'm not hurt."

Madison wanted to snap that Ford's shoulder said otherwise, but instead, he pressed his lips together.

He still didn't know where Ford stood. Initially, Madison had thought he was working with Antonio and the other people who'd taken Ashley. He'd been convinced Ford would eventually betray him, but instead, he'd found himself getting shot at. He'd helped Madison twice now, and it was only thanks to him that Madison was still breathing. That had to mean he wasn't working with the jaguars, right?

Madison looked up, but he was too afraid to ask. He didn't know what Ford's answer would be, and he didn't want to find out, at least not tonight.

"You don't know that they were after you and not me," Ford pointed out.

"I think we can assume they were after me. After all, I'm the one trying to find the temple, and I'm pretty sure those jaguars were part of the lost pride."

The expression on Ford's face told Madison he was right. Even if Ford wasn't a member of the pride, he knew about them. He knew they were after Madison.

Madison's heart broke a little, but he told himself not to be hurt. After all, he and Ford barely knew each other, and Ford didn't owe him anything. Whatever there was between him and the lost pride was none of Madison's business, and Ford had been keeping him alive. He hadn't betrayed Madison. He'd been doing his best dealing with the situation how he could, as had Madison.

"I'm not leaving you alone in the jungle," Ford said. "So you can stop asking. You can also stop worrying about my shoulder because I'm fine. It's just a scratch, and it'll heal soon."

"I never expected this to be such a disaster," Madison whispered. As it was, he'd even be happy to just find Ashley. He yearned to find the temple, but he'd lived all his life without being able to shift. It hurt, but he could survive going home like this.

He didn't want anyone to be hurt because of his obsession with getting his grandmother back. Ashley might already have been hurt, and Ford had been wounded. How many people would have to bleed for this? It was a legend, and while some kind of magic existed, Madison couldn't be sure that his dream of getting his grandmother back would ever come true. It sounded incredible, and maybe it was.

"You should go to sleep," Ford murmured.

Madison wanted to protest, but his eyelids were closing on their own, and he knew he wouldn't last much longer. He'd have to trust Ford to keep him safe tonight like he had last night. After what had happened today, he did, and it was easier to lie down on his pad and close his eyes.

Madison didn't know what was going on in Ford's mind, but Ford was on his side for now. Hopefully, that would continue until they got out of the jungle.

And if it didn't, well, Madison wouldn't blame him.

The jungle never fell silent. Ford listened to the sounds of the animals around them going about their night, his gaze never moving from Madison's sleeping figure. The man trusted him to keep him safe, yet he was about to betray him.

He swallowed and took out his satellite phone from his backpack. He'd had it from the beginning but hadn't used it yet. He hadn't had a reason to. Now, though, he did, and he wasn't looking forward to the call he had to make.

He was protecting Madison, or at least, that was what he told himself. He was protecting himself, too, and in the end, that was what mattered. Madison was nothing to him. They hadn't known each other before and weren't friends.

Yet, something ached in Ford as he quietly stepped away and turned on the phone.

He knew what he had to do. This was getting too dangerous for him, and he needed to cut his losses while he still could. That meant calling his brother and telling him he'd be handing Madison over.

Diego would probably scold Madison and explain to him that the temple was sacred, and Madison would understand. He had a good reason to want to find the temple, but he was a historian. He loved this shit, so he'd get it. He'd go back home, and Ford would never have to worry about him again.

He normally wouldn't have hesitated, but the betrayal tasted sour. He didn't want to hurt Madison, even though he didn't understand why. The wolf was nothing to him, and that was what he told himself as he dialed his brother's number.

"Ford? Do you know what time it is?" Diego asked when he answered.

"Yeah, sorry. I didn't think to check the time before calling."

"Is everything all right?"

Ford snorted. Diego sounded normal, but the situation was anything but. Diego had sent his people to shoot at Ford and Madison, and they could have died. How could he sound so normal after all of that was anyone's guess, and Ford didn't understand.

He supposed he didn't have to understand. He just had to do this in order to keep Madison safe.

"You know everything is not okay," Ford accused.

"Clearly, since you're calling me in the middle of the night. What's going on?"

"I'm giving up. I'll hand the professor over as long as you promise not to hurt him."

There was a moment of silence, and Ford listened to ensure Madison wasn't waking up. He was still softly snoring, though, so Ford relaxed.

"I have no idea what you're talking about."

The words stunned Ford. "You sent your people to shoot at us."

"I didn't send anyone anywhere. I don't even know where you are. I just know you're not home because your neighbor told me when I went over there yesterday."

The words didn't make sense. "I'm sure those were your pride members. They followed us to the jungle and attacked us twice. I even had to fight off one of your guys in my jaguar form."

"You're going to have to explain because I don't know what you're talking about."

Ford wanted to believe him. Diego wasn't a liar, and all of this had felt out of character. He cared for his pride, probably more than he cared for Ford, but that didn't mean he wanted Ford dead. If he needed something, he'd talk to Ford about it. If he hadn't wanted Ford to take Madison to the temple, he would have told him that to his face, not sent someone to kill him without even mentioning the issue.

But if he wasn't behind all of this, who was? Who were the people hunting Madison and Ford?

"I'm in the jungle right now," he explained, trying to think about what was safe to tell his brother. He wanted to blurt out everything but didn't need Diego to protect him. They were nothing to each other, even though they were brothers.

"You have a new client?"

"I do. Look, something weird is happening. People are hunting us and shooting at us, and I had to shift to fight."

"Why?"

"Because those guys are jaguars, and I didn't want to die."

There was a pause before Diego answered. "Are you telling me that my pride has attacked you?"

"I'm pretty sure they have. I didn't ask them if they were part of your pride, but they're jaguar shifters." And they were hunting Ford and Madison to stop them from getting to the temple. The only people who knew about it were part of Diego's pride.

Well, along with Ford and Madison.

"I have no idea what's happening, but I want you to come home. I need to know you're safe. Are you wounded? Do you need me to come to pick you up?"

Ford almost snorted again. "I'm fine. My client is freaking out, but he's not giving up, and he's going to get himself killed."

"Why would a hike through the jungle be so important to him?"

Ford had called his brother believing Diego already knew what was happening. He'd see this as a betrayal, but there was no way out of explaining why Ford and Madison were here.

Ford licked his lips. "He's a professor at some university back in the States. He was looking for the temple, and I told him I'd take him there."

The silence was even longer now. Ford wondered if Diego had hung up but knew he couldn't be so lucky. His brother would demand an explanation, and he'd be pissed. Even though Ford wasn't a pride member, they were still siblings, no matter how hard Ford was resisting that idea.

"Our secret temple? You agreed to take him there?"

"Look, he loves history and shit, and he's harmless. He's also looking for a friend of his that's disappeared, and I think the pride is involved. I thought you were and called you to beg for your mercy."

Diego sighed. "I have to look into this, but you can't take him to the temple, Ford. You know it's sacred."

Ford did, and while he didn't understand why people felt so strongly about the place, he couldn't deny that was the case. "I just want out."

"I can help you with that. I'll send someone to the town closest to you. Give me your position, and make sure you're there when they come to pick you up. We need to talk about this face-to-face, and you can't avoid it, so don't even try."

"I know." Ford *was* going to try, though. His brother meant well, but Ford was an asshole who didn't want to be berated like a child. He'd hand over Madison to whoever his brother sent, and then he'd be on his way. He should never have accepted this job, to begin with, but he could still make it out of the situation in one piece.

It went against everything he was to do this, but he didn't have a choice. He was in this for the money but wouldn't get paid if Madison got killed.

At this point, he doubted he'd get paid at all. Madison was going to be pissed when he found out what was happening, and for some reason, that broke Ford's heart.

But he told himself he didn't have a heart as he hung up with his brother. He was doing this so both he and Madison could survive, and even though Madison would be pissed, it wouldn't be Ford's problem. He'd already be far away, and he'd never see Madison again.

CHAPTER NINE

"There's a small town nearby. I know it's not what you want, but I think we should stop there, get a room for the night, and rest," Ford said.

He was eyeing Madison as if he expected him to say no. Madison was tempted to so he could see Ford's reaction, but in reality, he wanted to kiss the guy. "We can do that," he agreed.

Ford blinked. "You want to pause the search for the temple?"

"Considering we were chased twice since we entered the jungle, I think it's a good idea for us to take a day to rest." Madison would have killed for a shower and a bed. Hell, he would have killed for a bucket of cold water and a couch.

He needed to find the temple, and he hadn't changed his mind about finding and rescuing Ashley, but he wouldn't be any good if he was exhausted and couldn't think straight. Going to this town would waste the better part of the day, but Madison could deal with that. Maybe it would even help them lose the people who were after them.

They hadn't seen them since Ford had fought with one of them, and Madison hoped things stayed that way. He didn't care about who they were and why they were hunting them. He just needed them to stay as far away from him as possible.

Ford didn't look convinced, almost as if he expected Madison to tell him it was a joke and that they weren't going anywhere. They stared at each other for a moment, and Madison was pretty sure his smile was slightly manic. Was it that surprising that he wanted out of the jungle for a bit? The place wasn't exactly pleasant, even without bullets flying.

"It's this way," Ford gestured to the right.

They'd been exploring the last area left on Ashley's map, but they hadn't found anything so far. They had to be methodical because it would be easy for them not to see the ruins, even though it was a freaking temple. With the vegetation, it might be hidden by trees and bushes, and Madison didn't want to miss it just because he hadn't been thorough. It had slowed them down a lot, though. Between that and the fear that someone would kill them at any moment, Madison would be glad to have a good night's rest.

They changed direction, but Madison never stopped looking around for a hint of a stone wall.

For some reason, his thoughts kept drifting to Ford. Something was happening. He was especially distracted and jumpy today. Every time Madison talked to him, he looked guilty, which wasn't something Madison had thought he could feel. Ford was unabashedly himself, and he wasn't ashamed of it. He didn't hesitate to admit he was in this for the money and that he didn't care about the temple or what Madison wanted from it. He wanted to get paid, which was something Madison could understand.

Not everyone was obsessed like him. Not everyone had a life calling, and Madison himself might not have this one if it weren't for his grandmother and her stories. She was the main reason he'd gotten into this line of work, and he couldn't help but wonder what he'd do once all of this was over. If he found the temple and got her back, what would happen to his passion? It felt like a means to an end right now, like something that still linked them together, and he hoped he wouldn't lose it.

His passion for history would never go away. He might not need to explore this area of the world anymore, but that didn't mean he'd stop loving history.

But this wasn't something he needed to think about now.

They were silent as they walked, but Madison kept peeking at Ford. They were both distracted, which explained why Ford didn't see the hole. Madison didn't, either, but that wasn't a surprise. He seldom took an interest in the things around him.

He *did* notice it when Ford suddenly disappeared. There was a crash and a yelp, and Ford wasn't there anymore. Madison rushed toward him, frantically looking around. He didn't find Ford until he looked down.

He wasn't sure what had created the hole. Maybe it was the rain, or maybe some animal had dug it. Madison didn't think so, case because it was too big, but he expected anything from the jungle.

The hole was deep, so much so that even when Ford got to his feet, he couldn't reach the top. He looked around to find a way to climb, but the earth was slick with water. It hadn't rained since Madison had entered the jungle, but he knew it had a few days before he'd arrived in the country. The earth had soaked up the water, and the hole was damp, which made Ford grimace.

"I'm going to find a way out of this," he promised.

Madison got his backpack off his shoulders and nodded. "I know."

"I could shift."

Madison glanced at the hole. "I doubt you'll be able to do much. You won't be able to grab anything if you're in your jaguar form, and there's nothing for you to hold on to as you try to get out of the hole." Madison sucked in a breath. "I'll help you."

To his surprise, Ford looked hesitant. "You should continue walking. The town is just half an hour away, so if you stay in the right direction, you'll be there quickly. You can send help."

"You think I'm going to leave you here?"

"Why not? It would make sense for you to save yourself."

"There's nothing to save myself from." At least, not at the moment. Madison was sure the people who'd attacked them were still after them, but while he was terrified, it didn't mean he was going to abandon Ford. They were a team, even though he wasn't sure they liked each other most of the time.

He looked around, trying to find something that could help. He had rope in his backpack, which was the best thing he could use in this situation.

"You should go," Ford repeated. "What if those people find us?"

"Then I have to be quick getting you out of that hole. I can't fight for shit."

Ford laughed. He looked surprised that he had, but Madison liked the sound. He had a feeling Ford didn't laugh or smile often enough. A crazy part of him wanted to be the person who made that happen, but he wasn't an idiot. He'd be leaving the jungle eventually, but it was Ford's home, and he wasn't going anywhere. There was no future for them.

But that didn't mean he was leaving Ford in that hole.

He got the rope out of his bag and looked around. There were plenty of trees he could tie the rope around, so he quickly chose one that looked sturdy and wasn't too far away from the hole. As he worked, he could hear Ford trying to get out, but he fell back every time.

When Madison peeked into the hole again, it was to see Ford covered in mud from head to toe. Madison wrinkled his nose and dropped the rope down, already knowing he'd have to get dirty. At least there was a shower at the end of the day. They wouldn't have to use tissues to get clean and sleep on the ground.

"I tied it to a tree," he told Ford when Ford pulled on the

rope. "That way, even if I let go, it won't fall into your hole."

"Things don't fall into my hole," Ford muttered.

Madison's cheeks flamed. "Now's not the moment."

"Every moment is good to make sexual innuendos," Ford said with a wink.

Maybe Madison should leave him in the hole after all.

"I'm not as strong as you, so you're going to have to help," he warned as he positioned himself. He pressed his feet into the ground and wrapped the rope around his hands and forearms. He had no idea what he was doing, but he'd find out soon enough if it worked.

"Ready?" he asked.

"Ready," Ford confirmed.

Madison started pulling.

Ford had expected Madison to take the *out* when he'd offered it. He would have. The town was close enough that it would have been easy for Madison to get there and send someone to help while he got a room and enjoyed the luxury of a shower, but instead, he was helping Ford out of the mess he'd gotten himself into.

Ford had been distracted. That was the only explanation he could find for the fact that he hadn't noticed the hole. It was too late when he had, and his foot was already going down. It had encountered emptiness, and Ford had fallen forward.

His dignity hurt almost as much as his body. He knew he'd be bruised by the end of the day, and his shoulder kept reminding him that he was wounded, but if he wanted to do anything about it, he needed to get out of the hole. So, when Madison started pulling, Ford pushed up. He kept the rope securely around his waist and in his hands and used his knees and feet to climb.

It wasn't easy. The mud clung to his pants and was almost

too soft for him to use to push himself upward. He would have been stuck if it weren't for Madison pulling him along.

It was a miracle that Madison had enough strength to do that. Ford hadn't expected it, but he was starting to realize that he'd underestimated Madison, which wasn't something he usually did. He felt ashamed, especially considering why they were going into town.

He was handing Madison over to his brother.

What the fuck was he doing? If Madison knew what Ford was planning, he'd be gone. He would have abandoned Ford where he was, and he might not even have warned anyone about what had happened. Madison wasn't petty or anything like that, but he seemed to feel things so much more strongly than Ford ever had.

Except it was a lie. Ford felt things, and he felt them for Madison. It didn't make sense, but Ford supposed that emotions seldom did.

To be honest, nothing in this situation made sense.

"Come on," Madison said with a grunt.

Ford could see him now, and he risked unhooking one of his hands from the rope. He held it up, and Madison hesitated before grabbing it. His palm was warm and slick with sweat, but it felt like heaven in Ford's hand. They worked together until Ford finally got to the edge of the hole. He pushed himself up the last few inches, then quickly scrambled away from the ledge. He wasn't going to fall into the hole a second time.

He stayed on his hands and knees for a moment, breathing in and out. Madison stood next to him, his hands on his knees as he tried to catch his breath. They looked at each other, and Madison started laughing.

"Your face," he said.

Ford touched it, not one bit surprised to feel his face was caked with mud, too. He ran a fingertip down his cheek, then swiped it down Madison's, who squeaked and jumped back.

"Not fair. I got you out of that hole."

"And I thank you for that. You really should have left, though."

Madison shook his head. "I couldn't have. I knew I could help you, and I did."

"Well, thank you." Ford couldn't look away.

Madison's cheeks were flushed, and he was sweating. They both smelled, because they hadn't been able to shower in days and they'd been running. Madison's hair was all over the place, and his glasses kept slipping down his nose. His clothes were plastered to his body from the sweat, and his legs were caked with mud.

Yet Ford had never seen a more beautiful man.

That was all the explanation Ford could find for what happened next. He reached for Madison, maybe to swipe his finger over his cheek a second time, but that wasn't what happened. Instead, Ford cupped Madison's cheek. Madison's eyes widened, but he stepped closer, and when their lips met, Ford closed his eyes.

This was a bad idea. Madison wasn't staying, and Ford was about to hand him over to his brother. After he did that, Madison would hate him and want nothing to do with him.

But right now, he was solid in Ford's arms. His mouth tasted sweet, and he wasn't hesitant like Ford had expected him to be. For some reason, he hadn't thought Madison would be assertive, but he loved that he'd been wrong.

There was no hesitation in the way Madison moved. It was clear he wanted to kiss Ford and that he wasn't going to waste this opportunity, and neither was Ford. They wouldn't have a second chance at this after Ford handed Madison over.

He couldn't. He'd tried to convince himself to the contrary since he'd called Diego, but he'd always known he wouldn't be able to do it. Madison was too precious, and he was looking for the temple for a good reason. The old stories all mentioned that the temple was used for healing, and that was what Madison needed. It wouldn't be fair to keep him away, all in the name of secrecy. Ford couldn't be sure his brother would see things the same way, but he had to try. That meant not handing Madison over. Luckily, Ford had a plan for that.

Madison's arms wrapped around Ford's neck, and Ford pushed forward until he could press Madison against a tree. Madison jumped up, and Ford used his strength to hold him up as he wrapped his legs around him. Between that and the press of the tree, he was able to keep Madison up in his arms and devour his mouth.

Madison gave as good as he got. He wasn't the shy professor Ford had imagined in the beginning. He knew what he wanted, and just like when looking for the temple, he had no hesitation. He was passionate, and Ford wanted so much more than a kiss in the jungle.

But here, they were too exposed. The people hunting them could find them at any moment, and Ford was unwilling to put Madison in danger even more than he already had.

He was reluctant as he stepped away, especially when Madison made a wounded noise and tried to hold him close.

"We should go to town," Ford murmured. "I don't want the assholes with the guns to find us here."

Madison's eyes were hooded as he peered up at Ford. "When we get to whatever hotel you're taking me to, I want us to get only one room."

Ford swallowed. "I wouldn't have it any other way."

He'd have to find a way to stop Diego. Maybe he could call him once Madison was in the shower. Ford had no doubt he'd spend a bunch of time in there, and hopefully, that time would be enough for him to convince his brother not to come and to give Madison a chance.

That was all Madison and Ford needed. Madison needed a chance to be complete after having so many difficulties to shift all of his life, and Ford needed a chance to show Madison that even though he'd almost betrayed him, he cared about him.

Madison almost cried when he walked into the bathroom and saw the shower. The hotel wasn't much, but it felt like a palace after spending time in the jungle. The sheets on the bed appeared clean, as did the towels. When Madison grabbed one, it smelled of laundry soap, and the small stack of soap and shampoo bottle in the shower were calling his name.

He stripped and dropped his clothes on the floor. He'd deal with those later, although he doubted that washing them would do any good. They were a lost cause, but Madison would have to deal since he wasn't back home or even in Ashley's hotel room.

Not tonight, though. Tonight, the only thing he wanted to focus on was in the bedroom, waiting for his turn in the shower. Madison couldn't wait for them to get to what would come next, so even though he wanted to linger in the shower, he did a quick but thorough job that left the bathroom steamy and smelling of cleanliness.

Madison felt better. He'd probably start sweating again soon, but he could get another shower. Maybe he and Ford could take it together.

The thought made pleasure swirl in Madison's stomach. It had been a while since he'd been with anyone, and he wasn't sure he trusted Ford a hundred percent, but he liked him. They'd gone through a lot together, and it had brought them close. There was no way to know how close or where this would lead them, but that was a question Madison could obsess over later.

Right now, he had something better to do.

He couldn't put the clothes he'd worn when he'd entered

the bathroom back on, and he'd left his backpack in the bedroom. That meant he didn't have anything to wear when he went back to the bedroom, but did he need it? He and Ford were on the same page when it came to what was about to happen. Madison might as well already be naked.

The problem was that he wasn't sure Ford would like what he saw. Madison wasn't usually self-conscious, but that was because no one saw him naked. Considering the way Ford looked, he could have anyone he wanted. For some reason, he'd chosen Madison.

Madison told himself that if Ford decided he didn't want this, then he'd deal with it, but unless that happened, how he looked didn't matter. He wrapped his towel around his hips, straightened his back, and opened the door.

Ford was on the phone by the window, but he looked up when he heard the door. His lips opened, and he stared, making Madison want to run back into the bathroom. Instead, he made his way to the bed, feeling like an idiot and resisting the urge to cover himself.

"I have to go," Ford said. He hung up without waiting for an answer from whoever he'd been talking to.

"Your turn," Madison said. He sat on the edge of the mattress, then wondered if he should try to be more seductive. He'd just told Ford to shower, which wasn't nice, but neither of them could deny they stank after trekking through the jungle for days. Ford was covered in mud, and Madison wasn't looking forward to touching him in the state he was in.

Ford nodded. "Thank you. I'll be right back."

He almost ran to the bathroom, which made Madison uneasy. Was it because Ford didn't know how to tell him he'd changed his mind? Madison couldn't imagine it was because he was so eager to get into bed with him. No one ever was.

Madison didn't hate his body or anything like that, but he wasn't an idiot. He was a short guy who spent most of his days sitting in a chair. He looked average at best, probably worse after the past few days. There was little that was appealing about him, even though he wasn't repellent.

He sighed and got up to grab his backpack. His clean underwear was buried at the bottom, so he got most of his stuff out. He was too tired to put everything back where it belonged, so he left it there and slid into bed.

His body ached, and the first touch of the clean sheets against his skin made him sigh in pleasure. He didn't know what would happen next, but he couldn't remember being happier. He could finally sleep in a bed and not worry about someone shooting at him while he was unconscious.

He wasn't going to sleep just yet. He'd wait for Ford to come out of the bathroom.

Or at least, that was what he'd been planning on doing. When he snapped his eyes open, it was to the feeling of Ford slipping into bed next to him. He'd missed Ford coming out of the bathroom, which meant he'd fallen asleep.

Madison started to sit up, but Ford grabbed his shoulder and pulled him back down. "Where are you going?" he asked in a whisper as if he was afraid to send Madison running.

Madison didn't blame him because he was tempted to do just that. Instead, he stretched out on the mattress again, holding his breath.

"Have you changed your mind?" Ford asked in a stronger voice.

Madison was relieved the room was dark. It was easier to talk to Ford like this without being able to look him in the eyes. "No. Have you?"

A hand skimmed down Madison's chest, making him shiver. "No."

That was all Madison needed to feel stronger. Ford knew him. He'd seen him mostly naked. He still wanted him, and Madison wanted him back. Ford didn't move away when

Madison wrapped an arm around his neck or when Madison pushed closer to kiss him. He kissed Madison back, his lips warm and steady, and Madison forgot everything about what he looked like or whether or not Ford liked it.

He could feel the proof of that pressing against his thigh.

Neither of them had come prepared because they hadn't expected this to happen, but that was all right. Most of the time, when Madison was with someone, no penetration was involved, and besides, while he liked Ford more than he should, he still wondered if he could trust him fully.

But he didn't want to think about that right now. He was in Ford's arms, and he could imagine that they had a future together. He wanted to.

He'd always been so focused on his research and on finding the temple that he seldom felt lonely, but having Ford with him made him feel good. He wanted that feeling to continue, even though he didn't see a way to make that happen, but he wouldn't find one tonight. Tonight, they would share this, and it would be enough.

It felt like *everything*. Ford touched Madison as if he were precious, and it gave Madison hope that he felt that way.

His underwear quickly vanished somewhere in the bed. Madison had noticed Ford was already naked, and once they were skin to skin, his entire body flushed. Ford rolled Madison onto his back and never stopped kissing him as he settled between his legs. Madison opened them wide to make more space for him. Maybe it wasn't so bad that his body was softer than it should be. Ford didn't seem to care, and Madison decided he didn't, either.

He thrust his hips up as Ford pushed down. With their bodies pressed together like this, Madison could feel every one of Ford's movements, and he yearned for more. He clung to Ford's shoulders, exploring his broad back and arms with his fingers, shuddering at the feeling of so much power focused on him. Ford made him feel like the most important person in the world right now, which wasn't something that happened often. Ford's hands felt like they were everywhere, while at the same time, his mouth drove Madison nuts. Ford's body was heavy on top of Madison, yet it felt perfect, and they moved in unison as if they'd been doing this for years.

Madison never wanted it to end, but that was impossible, and as he felt the pleasure take over, he promised himself he'd give Ford a chance.

He didn't know what his future held, but he could only hope—his grandmother back with him, a job he enjoyed, and maybe a relationship with Ford.

CHAPTER TEN

When Madison opened his eyes, he was already smiling, and he doubted he'd be able to stop anytime soon.

He couldn't believe it. Well, he could, because his ass ached from what he and Ford had done last night. It was a reminder he knew he'd feel once they started walking again.

He didn't mind. He'd wanted this more than he'd admitted even to himself. He'd tried keeping his distance from Ford, but how could he? In the beginning, Ford had seemed like he didn't care, but Madison had seen the signs as that changed. He wasn't sure anything would have happened between them if Ford hadn't needed Madison to show him that he could rescue him as well as he could rescue Madison, but that didn't matter. It had happened, and they'd ended up in bed together.

And it had been delicious.

Madison didn't fool himself into thinking they had any kind of future. He had his life and work back home, while Ford belonged in the jungle. Madison would never ask him to leave it, and he was trying to convince himself not to worry too much about the future. It would find them even if he didn't, and he wanted to enjoy the little time he had with Ford. Besides, he didn't know what he'd want to do after finding the temple. He didn't love teaching, so maybe he could find something else that would bring him closer to Ford.

"You're thinking so loudly I can hear you," Ford mumbled against his pillow.

"At least I *can* think."

Ford opened an eye and glared. "Are you saying I'm too stupid to think?"

Madison grinned. "I just meant that you're a much more physical person than I am."

Ford wiggled his eyebrows. "You didn't seem to mind last night."

Madison's cheeks flushed, but there was nothing to be ashamed of. He hadn't minded last night and wouldn't mind this morning, either.

He leaned forward, pressing his lips against Ford's. He didn't think about morning breath until it was too late, but Ford didn't seem to care. He kissed Madison back in a slow rhythm that made Madison ache for more.

"Can we stay here for a bit longer?" he eventually asked as he dropped back against the pillow.

Ford moved closer, arching a brow. "Don't you want to find your temple?"

"Of course I want to find it. I . . ." Madison hadn't told Ford the entire truth about the temple and what he hoped he'd find, but it was time.

He sat up and tried to find the best way to explain that he hoped that an artifact most people didn't think existed had the power to bring people back from death and that he hoped to use it.

"The reason I love history so much is that my grandmother used to tell me and my sister stories when we were kids. We spent a lot of time with her because both our parents worked, and I was very close to her." Madison licked his lips. "She told me about the lost pack and their temple and about the magic that people came from hundreds of miles away to see. She said it had the ability to heal, but also to bring people back from death, although only a handful of people were ever allowed to use it that way."

Madison couldn't stop thinking about it. He was so close

he could taste it, and he was starting to freak out. He had no idea how the magic worked or even if it *would* work after all this time had passed, but he had hope. He hadn't done all of this for nothing to happen.

Ford was quiet, but then, he usually was, so Madison wasn't worried. He couldn't stop thinking about his return home with his grandma and how he'd stun his family. His mother would freak out, and she'd demand to know how Madison had done it. He wasn't sure he wanted to tell her. She loved him, and she'd done her best, but she hadn't always been supportive. He also wasn't sure she'd believe him when he explained it was thanks to an ancient artifact. She didn't like his job and his area of expertise, and she always complained that he should have been a doctor or lawyer. She often said that if he'd been a doctor, he might have found a way to fully heal and finish growing, but Madison couldn't find it in himself to care about any of that now, even though it had hurt in the past.

He only cared that his grandma would be back with him soon.

"That sounds like a nice legend," Ford said.

"I hope it's not a legend. My grandmother died a few years ago."

Ford was silent for a moment. "And you want to bring her back from death? You have to see that's not possible, Madison."

Madison wasn't surprised Ford didn't believe in the legend. Some days, he wasn't sure he did, either. "I'm going to try."

"All right. I guess it doesn't change what we have to do."

Ford's reaction wasn't as enthusiastic as Madison had hoped, but at least he wasn't telling him he was crazy, so there was that.

The sooner they could get back into the jungle, the sooner

he'd find the temple, so while he wanted to stay in bed with Ford forever, he rolled to the side to get up.

An arm hooked around his waist, and Ford pulled him back. Madison didn't resist and fell against Ford's chest, a smile on his lips.

"What? I thought you wanted to go."

Ford kissed Madison's shoulder. "I do because I know this is important to you, but surely, we can take advantage of this bed for a while longer."

"It depends. What do you have in mind?"

Ford's soft smile widened. "So many things, and I'm not letting you out of bed until I've done them all to you."

Madison's entire body flushed. "I never want this to end," he whispered.

He pressed his face against Ford's neck, not wanting Ford to see the vulnerability in him. He probably shouldn't tell Ford how he felt about him, but he wasn't sure he could resist. He had feelings for Ford and couldn't do anything about it. He'd tried to resist, but the jaguar shifter had found his way under his skin, and Madison suspected there would be no getting him out of there anytime soon.

Ford ran his hand down Madison's bareback. "Me neither." He hesitated, and Madison was surprised when he pushed on. "I never expected anything like this to happen. I never expected *you* to happen."

"Well, I happened."

"You did," Ford confirmed. "And I'm not sure how I'm going to move on once you go home."

Madison peered up. "Maybe I don't have to go back home."

"And what would you do here? You're a professor, not a jungle guide."

That much was true, at least for the moment. "I don't think I can ever do what you do, but I never wanted to teach. I don't like people on the best of days, and young adults are annoying."

"Why do you do it, then?"

"Because it gave me the opportunity to research and come here for months over the summer. I don't know what I'll do if this works, but my life will change. Maybe I don't have to get back to teaching."

"What would you do, then?"

"I don't know, but I'll have time to decide what I want. I'm not saying I'll be moving here permanently soon, but it's an option."

Madison's heart raced as he wondered if he'd exposed himself too much. What if Ford shot him down? Maybe this was just an opportunity to have a little fun for him. Neither of them had been planning to spend the rest of their lives together until Madison had opened his big mouth. He still wasn't sure that was what he wanted, but he hoped he'd at least have the opportunity to explore the option.

"I wouldn't say no to having you closer," Ford murmured as he kissed Madison's shoulder again. "How about we talk again once you've found your temple and gotten what you want?"

He was right. That had to be Madison's priority, and it was, even though he'd allowed Ford to distract him—and he'd continue to allow it until they were both sick of being in bed.

But Ford had given him an in. He wasn't pushing him out of bed or his life, and even if things didn't work, right now, Madison knew they were both willing to try.

Ford didn't want to go back to reality yet, but he and Madison needed to eat. He left Madison in bed, looking rumpled and comfortable, and headed downstairs to grab food and a few items they'd need if they intended to spend the day in bed.

They did. They didn't have much time because Ford hadn't been able to convince Diego to stay back, but he'd been careful. No one knew they were here, and even if Diego's people got to the small town where they were hiding, it would take them a while to find them. Ford and Madison would leave in the early afternoon after Ford made sure they were safe and no one was following them, but they could take the morning to rest.

Or have sex.

Madison was nothing like Ford had thought. He was a nerdy professor, but he was also warm and caring. He bitched a lot, but he'd been there for Ford when he'd needed him and when anyone else would have left him in that hole.

And Ford had betrayed him.

Normally, he wouldn't have thought twice about that. He didn't care about anyone but himself, or at least, that was what his mother always told him. She was usually right about that, but there was something about Madison that had touched Ford, and he couldn't shake him anymore. Their night together was the first time in a while that Ford could remember actually caring about someone, and he was afraid to think about what would happen when this was over.

It would take a while yet. Diego had yelled at Ford last night when he'd told him he'd changed his mind. He'd promised he hadn't been the one to send the guys who'd attacked them twice and that he was looking into it, but Ford didn't know if he could believe that. Diego was the alpha of the pride. He knew everything that happened in it, or at least, he was supposed to. If he hadn't sent those guys, who had? And why? Was it only to stop Madison from finding the temple? Were they behind Madison's friend's disappearance?

They wanted to keep Madison away from the temple, but Ford didn't understand why. There was no way the whole *bring-people-back-from-the-dead* thing was real. It was just a bunch of old stone as far as he knew, but he wasn't part of the pride and didn't have all the info. Diego was supposed to, and if he really wasn't involved, Ford hoped he'd find the people who were and that he'd stop them from hurting Madison.

Ford couldn't let Diego take Madison anywhere until he was sure he wasn't behind all of this. In the meantime, he'd protect Madison to the best of his ability and do what he could to find the temple. Maybe if they found it before those guys caught them, Madison would have the time to figure things out. Ford didn't believe in the power of the temple, but Madison did, and that was what mattered.

Ford didn't waste time. As soon as he had food and lube — finding that hadn't been the best experience of his life considering how small the town was — he headed back to the hotel. It was tiny and tucked out of the way on a small street that ended where the jungle started, which would give Ford and Madison the advantage if they had to run again. Hopefully, they wouldn't have to do so today because Ford had plans.

Back at the hotel, he climbed the stairs two by two. His stomach churned, which was something that he wasn't used to. Sex was always casual for him, but there was nothing casual about Madison. He'd wiggled his way under Ford's skin with his bitching and adorableness. It didn't feel like those two things should fit together, but they did, and Madison was perfect.

Perfect for Ford.

It was terrifying. Ford had no idea how to deal with any of this, but considering their situation, maybe he didn't have to figure things out right away. Maybe he could just see what happened and focus on keeping Madison safe and helping him find the temple. Once that was over, they could worry about what was next, but it would be useless to do so now.

Ford sucked in a breath when he reached the room he shared with Madison, but he didn't hesitate to open the door.

He wasn't surprised to find Madison in bed with his eyes closed as he peacefully slept. He wasn't used to traipsing around the jungle, no matter what he did in the summer. It was nothing next to what he'd gone through these past few days, and it had taken its toll on him. He needed rest more than anything, but unfortunately, they couldn't linger here if he wanted to find the temple.

Ford closed the door as softly as he could, but the sound was still enough to make Madison jerk into a sitting position. He blinked, then relaxed when he saw Ford standing there.

"You got food?" he asked as he made grabby hands.

It made Ford smile. *He* made Ford smile, which wasn't something a lot of people could say. Ford raised the bag containing the food. "I did."

"What are you waiting for, then?" Madison grabbed his glasses from the nightstand and put them on. "I'm so hungry I could eat a horse."

"No horses, but this should be enough." Ford hadn't been sure what Madison liked, so he'd grabbed a bit of everything, which meant it was too much food. They might as well enjoy it, though, if they were going back to the jungle soon.

They sat on the bed, Madison still naked and only covered by the sheet pooled at his lower body, Ford wearing his pants and shirt. He'd removed his shoes but hadn't been sure about the rest and figured it could wait.

Eventually, Madison leaned back and patted his stomach. "That was the most delicious food I've ever eaten."

"It wasn't that good."

"Yeah, it was." Madison looked Ford up and down. "You're overdressed for this."

"For what?"

"Dessert."

Madison pushed away from his pillow and grabbed Ford's shirt. Ford went willingly, allowing Madison to stretch out on his back and pull until he was on top of him. Madison spread his legs wide, and Ford settled there like he belonged.

He wanted to. He wanted to be the person Madison reached for when he needed something. It wasn't like Ford, but he could already tell he'd do a lot of things that weren't like him when it came to Madison, and he was surprisingly okay with that.

Madison kissed him. Ford didn't give him his weight because he wanted to be naked when he did that. Instead, he pushed away, grinning when Madison chased his lips. He pouted, but Ford winked at him and unbuttoned his shirt.

"I like where you're going," Madison drawled.

"You'll like it even more when you see what's in that bag," Ford said, tilting his chin toward the plastic bag containing the lube.

Madison snatched it and peered inside, then took off his glasses and pushed away the sheet covering him. Ford couldn't look away as Madison opened his legs and took the lube out of the bag. He continued getting undressed while staring at Madison, who seemed unashamed of how exposed he was. He didn't hesitate to open the lube and slick his fingers, and by the time Ford was naked, he had two fingers inside himself.

Ford climbed back onto the bed. Madison started to withdraw his fingers, but Ford wanted to see more of that, so he lay between Madison's legs with his face hovering over Madison's cock. Madison got the hint and continued what he was doing, and Ford focused on the hard cock in front of his face. He didn't think Madison needed more stimulation, but that didn't mean he wouldn't give it to him.

He wrapped his lips around Madison's cock. Madison's legs tightened around Ford, and the rhythm of his fingers stuttered, which spurred Ford to continue what he was doing. He didn't think he could do it for long, but they'd have other occasions. Ford couldn't think they wouldn't.

"How long are you going to make me wait?" Madison asked breathlessly.

Ford popped off his cock to look up at him. "I'm tempted to make you come like this."

"And I'm tempted to hit you."

Ford laughed. "I didn't know you were into that."

Madison reached for Ford's arms and pulled him up. "I'm into many things you'll only learn about if you stick around."

He'd been tentative yesterday when he'd mentioned this, and they both knew it wouldn't be easy, but maybe it wasn't impossible. They'd have to compromise, and neither of them could make promises, but they didn't have to right now. They just needed to be together, so Ford moved up Madison's body to kiss him.

Madison welcomed him, wrapping himself around him as if he was afraid Ford might run. Ford wasn't going anywhere, though, and as he slid into Madison, he knew he'd always feel that way. He didn't know what to make of that, but it was easy not to think about it when Madison arched his back and pushed Ford deeper into his body.

The future was terrifying, but with Madison, Ford felt just a little bit less afraid.

CHAPTER ELEVEN

"Did you pack everything?"

Madison looked around the room. He still wanted to find the temple but wasn't looking forward to leaving the hotel. He and Ford had been in a bubble for the past day and night, and it wasn't easy to leave it, especially since Madison didn't know what would happen next.

He and Ford hadn't made any promises to each other. Well, Ford had promised to help Madison find the temple, but they didn't know what would happen next. Madison would have to go home eventually, and Ford's home was here.

But for now, Madison wasn't going anywhere except to the temple. He'd figure out how the magic worked, grab Ashley, and get her out of whatever situation she was in. Hopefully, the people after him had decided he'd gotten lost in the jungle. He didn't fancy getting shot at again, so he hoped it wouldn't happen.

Madison sighed. "Yeah, I have everything."

Ford kissed his cheek. "Everything will be all right."

Madison wanted to believe him, but he wasn't sure he could. There was too much at stake, and they didn't have all the information they needed. They still had no idea why those people had shot at them and were after them, but it had to be related to the temple.

Considering that the people after them were shifters, maybe they were guarding the temple. Maybe they were trying to stop Madison from getting there and using the magic. Wouldn't it be easier for them to talk to Madison, though? He could be reasoned with. Sure, he wanted to use the magic, but he didn't know if he could or if it was even real. He'd have given all of it up if it meant saving Ashley. Those people had never attempted to contact him, though. They'd taken Ashley, had shot at Madison, and had tried to kill him.

The sound of a door slamming and a woman screaming somewhere in the hotel made Madison jump. He looked at the door with wide eyes but didn't ask what was happening. Ford was here with him, so he didn't know, either.

Ford's smile was gone. It was clear he thought something was going on, too, and it probably wasn't good.

"What do we do?" Madison asked.

Ford eyed the door for a moment longer, then, to Madison's surprise, pulled him toward the window.

"What are you doing?" Madison asked.

"I think they found us."

"It could be unrelated. It was just a door slamming."

"And a woman screaming."

"Maybe she saw a spider or something."

Ford cocked his head, turning to look at Madison. "Do you scream like that when you see a spider?"

Madison would never admit that he did, so he shook his head. "Maybe something else happened."

"And I'm ready to bet that something else is that they found us. Come on. It'll be safer for us to leave through the window."

"Are you sure about that?" Madison eyed the small street on which the window gave. "Because I'm pretty sure I'm going to end up splattered on the ground."

"I'll make sure you don't."

Ford made it look easy. After opening the window, he swung both of his legs on the other side of it. There was a tiny ledge, and while Ford fit on it, Madison was pretty sure he wouldn't. He was too big for that, and he glared down at his stomach, berating himself for eating so much at breakfast.

Ford's hand appeared. "Come on. We need to go."

Something in his voice told Madison he had a reason to be worried. "Why? What's happening?"

Ford wiggled his fingers, and Madison took them. He leaned out the window, sucking in a breath when he saw the two cars in front of the hotel. Two guards stood next to them, holding guns.

Madison and Ford had been found.

Ford would never leave Madison alone, but he was only one man. He wouldn't be able to fight however many people were trying to get to them, and Madison didn't want him to try. He wanted Ford to be safe, which wouldn't happen if they stayed here. Ford was right.

They needed to leave through the window.

Madison looked out again. The ledge was tight, but there was an awning under it. It wasn't big, but it would cushion the fall if Madison were to fall.

He wasn't sure how else he and Ford would get out of the situation. The ledge outside the window didn't lead anywhere. They would have to find a way to climb down, and Madison wasn't looking forward to it.

But he still took Ford's hand and clambered out the window.

His heart was in his throat, but he told himself it wasn't that high. Even if he fell, he'd probably be okay. Even though he'd never been able to easily shift, he was a shifter, which meant his body was sturdier than a normal human's. It had to be to withstand the many shifts, no matter how tortuous they were. Madison was more resistant to getting broken than a human.

He was about to find out just how much.

He plastered his back against the hotel's outside wall and did his best not to look down as he and Ford moved sideways. They weren't holding hands anymore because they couldn't, but Ford wasn't far. It helped Madison to know he was there, going through the same things as him. He was trying to save Madison, something not many people would have done. After all, the guys with the guns weren't after Ford. They were after Madison, and anyone in their right mind would have handed him over and washed their hands of him.

But not Ford. They might not have made any promises to each other, but they were in this together.

"We're going to have to jump," Ford eventually said.

"We're going to break something."

"Maybe, but it'll be better than getting shot at."

"Will it? Because I'm pretty sure that both of those things hurt like hell."

Ford grabbed Madison's hand again. "Do you trust me?"

"We're not on a fucking ship, Ford." Ford looked confused, and Madison shook his head. "Never mind. I was referencing a movie. We're going to get hurt or maybe even die. I don't want to do this."

"We might get hurt, but I'm not letting anyone shoot you."

Madison was terrified, but he didn't think they had a choice. He nodded at Ford as he heard the door of their hotel room open. The sound of footsteps rushing in gave him the boost he needed. Ford seemed to feel the same way because he jumped, taking Madison with him.

They had to be discrete, which meant Madison couldn't scream. He bit on his lower lip hard enough to draw blood, but he and Ford landed before he could worry about it. The air whooshed out of Madison's lungs, and he struggled to breathe as he slid down the awning. It was a miracle it hadn't ripped under their weight, or at least he thought so until he felt it start to do just that.

His eyes went wide, and he just had the time to suck in a breath before the awning ripped under him. Thankfully, it had been sturdy enough to break their fall, and even though

Madison's ass hurt where he landed on it, he was in one piece.

Mostly.

Ford was already up and running, pulling Madison along. Madison could only go with him, darting around the two cars and the guys standing by them. They were so stunned they didn't react for the first few seconds, and that gave Ford and Madison enough time to reach the dead end of the small street.

Madison had thought Ford had chosen this hotel on purpose. It was small and out of the way, and more importantly, so close to the jungle that it only took them a handful of minutes to reach it.

"I don't like any of this," Madison grumbled.

"You'd like being dead even less," Ford told him.

He never slowed down, and Madison didn't dare ask him to. He could hear people shouting behind them, which probably meant the guys with the guns were coming. Hopefully, they'd lose them in the jungle, but there was a chance they wouldn't.

Madison was so fucking ready for all of this to be over.

"I'll keep you safe," Ford said as they ran.

His words were what made Madison realize how serious he was about Ford. He did trust Ford to keep him safe, even though they'd met only days ago. It felt like so much longer, and as he ran faster, he told himself that maybe they did have a chance.

As long as they made it out of the jungle with no bullet holes in their bodies.

Ford didn't know how long they ran, but he wanted to put as much space between them and the guns as possible. He was tempted to stop, grab the satellite phone, and call his brother, but he didn't dare. Even though he couldn't hear anyone behind them anymore, he didn't trust that they were just being discrete.

So they ran. Ford wanted to scream at Diego and ask him why he was hunting Madison, but he already knew the answer to that question. Diego wanted to stop Madison from finding the temple, and clearly, he was ready to do anything to obtain that. Maybe Ford should have told him why Madison was looking for the temple. He'd planned on calling Diego again before leaving the hotel, but it was too late. Diego had made his move, and now, the only thing Ford could do was run.

Things would be easier if he were alone, but he wasn't about to leave Madison behind. They were in this together, no matter how hard it was for Ford to believe. Madison was special, and Ford had stopped wondering what he saw in him. It didn't matter when he only wanted Madison to find the temple, use its magic, and be happy.

"I have to stop," Madison said after a while.

He'd been doing his best to keep up, but he was flushed and panting, and it was as if the past day and night in the hotel hadn't happened. They were right back to square one, in the same position they'd been in before reaching the small town.

"The farther we get, the better it is," Ford said.

Madison stumbled, and while Ford managed to keep him upright, Madison shook his head and pushed him away. "I get that, but it's not going to help if I can't move. I need to stop."

Ford had to go along with it. He paused, cocking his head as he listened to the jungle. He could hear animals and insects, but no one was shooting, and there was no sound of someone running now that he and Madison were still.

"Not for long," Ford warned.

"I don't need long." Madison flopped against a tree. He

didn't sit down, even though Ford was pretty sure he was dying to do just that. Instead, he pressed his hands to his knees and tilted his head forward.

"Stay here. I'm going to go back just a bit to make sure no one's coming," Ford said.

Madison turned wide eyes at him. "You can't leave me."

Ford kissed the top of Madison's head. He was sweaty, but Ford didn't care. "I'm not going far."

Madison looked like he wanted to protest, but he nodded instead, and Ford stepped away.

He had his phone out before he was out of sight, but it didn't matter because Madison had closed his eyes. He turned the phone on, and since he couldn't call Diego, he texted him.

What the fuck are you doing? I told you Madison doesn't mean the pride any harm and that I changed my mind about you taking him, but you sent people after us anyway.

Ford didn't expect an answer right away, but clearly, he'd caught his brother with his phone in his hand.

That man needs to be kept away from the temple.

Why? What do you think he's going to do, hide it in his bag and steal it from you?

This isn't funny, Ford. Tell me where you are and stay there.

Ford snorted. *I'm not telling you anything. I'll take him to the temple because he needs and deserves it.* If the temple's magic really did what Madison hoped it did, then Ford wanted him to have that.

What do you mean?

"Ford?" Madison called out before Ford could answer.

Ford hesitated, but eventually, he turned off the phone and put it in his backpack. He didn't think Diego would understand even if he knew why Madison needed the temple, and it wasn't Ford's explanation to give. He didn't think Madison shared his memories of his grandmother with many people, and while he might agree that Ford could tell Diego about it to save them, it wasn't needed.

Ford made his way back to Madison, relieved to see he was all right and not as out of breath as he'd been minutes earlier.

"I didn't see anyone," he told Madison.

"That's good. They're still coming after us, though, right?"

"I'm pretty sure they won't stop until they catch us."

Madison chewed on his lower lip. "Do you think they're guarding the temple?"

"It's possible, and it would make sense."

"Maybe they think I want to steal something."

"Maybe." Ford hooked an arm around Madison's shoulders and pulled him close. "They would know that's not the case if they hadn't started shooting. They could have talked to you, but instead, they decided to assume you had the worst intentions, and they're not giving you a chance to explain. I don't care what people want or think if they go straight to trying to kill you. As far as I'm concerned, they don't deserve the temple and whatever magic it has."

Madison didn't look convinced. Ford was pretty sure that if his friend hadn't vanished, he'd have thought about leaving without finding the temple. He respected history and the pride so much that he was ready to give up his dream of shifting.

But Ford had no respect for anyone, not even his brother, after what Diego had done. He'd give Madison what he wanted and didn't care how many people he had to mow down to make that happen.

He kissed Madison's cheek. "Come on. The temple isn't going to find itself."

Madison hesitated, but eventually, he nodded. "Where do we start?"

"By finding out where we are exactly." And from there, by going back to the only area on the map that Ashley hadn't explored yet. If the temple existed, it would be there.

And Ford and Madison would find it.

Chapter Twelve

When Madison saw the first stone, his gaze passed over it as if it wasn't out of place this deep in the jungle. It took his brain a moment to make sense of what he was seeing, and when it did, he sucked in a breath and reached out to grab Ford's arm.

Ford immediately stopped moving and looked around.

"What is it? Have they found us?"

They'd been running for a few days now. The night they'd spent at the hotel felt like a distant dream, even though they curled up together every evening under the stars. Sleeping on the hard ground in the jungle was far from comfortable, even with Ford by his side, but Madison was dealing with it. Having Ford with him made it easier, but Madison was still tired and hungry and, most of the time, afraid for his life.

The guys with the guns hadn't found them again after they'd run from the hotel. Madison didn't think they'd given up, which meant that every time he heard a branch crack — which unfortunately happened often in a jungle full of birds and animals — he thought they'd finally found him and Ford. He didn't know what they'd do when it happened, but he knew it wouldn't be good and wasn't looking forward to it.

He wasn't looking forward to a lot of things, and strangely, that included finding the temple.

But he was pretty sure it was too late for that.

He gestured at the stone he could see peeking from the vegetation on the ground. "Look."

"What is it?"

"I don't know." Madison stepped closer. He was careful as he pushed away leaves and debris from the stone. It was man-made, and there was another stone next to it, then another. Looking ahead, he could see they formed a path. Most of them were hidden under the earth and vegetation, but there were enough of them visible that Madison knew they'd done it.

They'd found the temple.

He got to his feet. His entire body trembled, and he was afraid to open his mouth because he didn't know what would come out of it. He was pretty sure he might start crying if he tried speaking, which wasn't something he wanted to do in front of Ford. Ford had seen Madison at his worst, sleeping on the ground and stinking from having walked for days in the jungle. Madison's skin itched because of the insect bites, and he could have killed for another shower.

But all of the disappointment and discomfort flew out the window when he realized they'd done it.

"Careful," Ford said when Madison stumbled forward. "We don't know what kind of protection the pride has in place."

That was enough to stop Madison from rushing ahead. "You think they're going to try to kill us again?"

"They have before, and if they realize we found their temple, they're not going to be happy."

"But it's abandoned. They wouldn't have abandoned it if they cared so much about it."

Ford shook his head. "I don't know that it's abandoned."

He was right. So far, Madison had only found a pathway. Even if he squinted, he couldn't see the temple ahead because of the trees and everything else, so he couldn't know what state it was in.

"We're almost there," he said. "I'm not going back."

"I never expected you to. I just need you to be careful."

"I will be." Madison took Ford's hand. "We both will."

There was a warning in his voice, and he was relieved when Ford nodded. Madison didn't only need him so he could get out of the jungle. He needed Ford to be okay as much as Ford needed him to be, so he understood.

Together, they followed the pathway. It wasn't always easy to see it, but eventually, they didn't need it anymore to find the temple because it was right in front of them.

Madison recognized the place from the pictures Ashley had sent. She'd found the same pathway and had followed it like Madison and Ford were. Madison wondered if she'd been as excited as he was. Probably, at least until the guys with the guns had found her. Madison was almost afraid to find the temple. What if Ashley was still here? What if those people had killed her and left her body inside?

But that didn't make sense. If the temple was sacred, they wouldn't abandon a body in it. Madison needed to stop letting his imagination freak him out and focus on what was in front of him.

The temple.

He and Ford were slow as they walked around it, mostly because it would be impossible to be faster. Too many things stood in their way, like rocks, trees, and bushes. Eventually, though, they found an entrance. It was dark, but when Madison peeked inside, he could see some light streaming in.

"This is the main entrance," Madison said as he pressed a hand against one of the stone columns that framed it. It was smooth and cool.

"Is there another one?" Ford asked. He kept looking around as if he expected something to happen.

Madison couldn't blame him. He expected something to happen, too. He just hoped it wouldn't be more people shooting at him. "They usually had more than one entrance, yes. One was for the people who came to pray to the gods and ask for their help, and another was for the people who worked here."

"Which one will be safer?"

Madison didn't understand the question. "This one looks safe enough. I mean, some of the stones of the wall have come down, but the entrance is sturdy."

Ford didn't look convinced. Madison wanted to give him time, but he couldn't resist. He was in front of the temple he'd been looking for his entire life. If everything went the way it should, he'd finally be able to shift in just a few minutes.

He took a step forward, then another. The temple was hidden by climbing trees and vegetation, but now that Madison was close enough, he could see it better. It looked incredibly intact for having been abandoned so long ago, and as he stepped into the cool, dark main room, he shivered.

This was too well preserved. Considering how long it had been, the temple shouldn't be in such a good condition. Now that he was inside, Madison could see someone regularly cared for it. They didn't cut trees, maybe to keep the temple hidden, but there was an obvious patch on the wall to Madison's right, and the floor was spotless.

The room he was in was wide, opening directly on what looked like an altar at the center. A round hole in the ceiling above it let the sunlight in, which was the main reason the room wasn't dark. The beam of sunlight fell straight on the altar, making it look magical.

Madison was fascinated. Was the hole there for that purpose or to give light to the room?

"I was starting to think you wouldn't find the temple," a man said.

His voice echoed in the room, and Madison took a step back, trying to locate him. Ford was behind him, and he pressed a hand against the small of Madison's back as if to warn him. They turned to run, only to find that someone was standing in the door from which they'd just come in.

They were trapped.

Madison looked around, trying to find the smaller entrance he'd told Ford about, but of course, the man talking to them had come from somewhere. He was standing by the entrance, leaning against the wall as he stared at them.

Madison didn't think he'd ever seen him before. He couldn't remember what the guys who'd shot at him looked like, though, so he might be wrong.

The man pushed away from the wall and moved closer. Madison scrambled back, telling himself that Ford would protect him, but would he? He was only one man against an alpha who probably had half his pride waiting outside.

"What are you doing here?" Ford asked.

He was staring at the man, and he didn't look surprised. Angry, and maybe a little scared, but not surprised.

The man stopped when he was closer. "I told you I couldn't allow anyone to find the temple. That includes your boyfriend." The man looked at Madison. "My name is Diego, and I'm the alpha of what you probably know as the lost pride." His gaze flickered to Ford. "I'm also Ford's brother."

Madison sucked in a breath. Pain seized his chest, and for a moment, he couldn't breathe.

Diego was the alpha of the lost pride, and Ford was his brother.

What the fuck was happening?

Madison took a step away from Ford, who reached for him. Madison didn't allow him to touch him. He was pretty sure he'd break down if he did, and he couldn't afford for that to happen. He was strong, and he didn't need Ford's support.

Hopefully.

"You could have made this easier on everyone," Diego scolded. "You should have stayed at the hotel and handed him over like we talked about."

Ford's hands had balled up into fists. He looked like he

wanted to hit the alpha, which confused Madison. If they were working together, why would Ford want that? Shouldn't he be happy that this was finally over and that he wouldn't have to worry about Madison anymore?

Madison was missing so many things, and he wanted answers, but he didn't think he'd be able to hear them over the sound of his heart breaking.

Ford had betrayed him. He'd known all along that the lost pride was real and still existed and that they probably protected the temple. Had he known where the temple was? Had he been leading Madison around the jungle just because he wanted to be paid? It was clear the end goal had always been to stop Madison from reaching the temple, but for some reason, they'd gotten here anyway.

"I told you I wouldn't hand him over," Ford said in a hard voice. "Madison, you have to believe me. I didn't know he'd be here. I thought we'd come in, you'd do your thing, and we'd be able to leave."

Madison shook his head. "How can I believe you?" Ford had lied to him, which meant Madison couldn't.

The last intact piece of his heart shattered.

Ford could see the heartbreak in Madison's expression, and he wanted to kick himself and Diego for hurting Madison like that. He needed to fix this, but how?

He'd lied to Madison. He hadn't told him about the pride, about Diego, or about being related to him. Did Diego *have* to open his big mouth the way he had? Ford couldn't remember the last time they'd brawled, but he was tempted to kick his brother in the nuts.

"I won't let you touch him," he said.

"You don't make the decisions here, Ford." Diego looked disappointed and angry, but so was Ford.

Diego always touted that they were brothers and should help each other, yet he was betraying Ford. His people had tried to kill Ford, and now, he was here to stop Madison. Did he think Ford wouldn't react if he hurt Madison? Maybe he did. Ford had never cared about anyone but himself, so Diego probably didn't expect him to care about Madison. Ford was still trying to make sense of his feelings, so it wasn't a surprise that Diego couldn't see what was right in front of his eyes.

But Ford wasn't done yet. He might not be able to give Madison what he needed from the temple, but he could make sure he didn't get hurt.

He grabbed Madison's hand and pulled him toward the entrance. There was someone there, but Ford barely slowed down enough to punch the man in the face. The man's nose made a crunching sound, and he grabbed for his face, so Ford kicked him in the nuts — it wasn't as satisfying as it would have been if it had been Diego — and ran past him. He heard Diego call out for him, but he didn't turn to see what his brother wanted.

He already knew Diego needed him to bring Madison back so they could make sure the professor wouldn't tell anyone about the temple. They'd make him disappear the way they had with his friend, and the world would be so much worse without Madison.

Ford wouldn't let that happen.

So, they ran. Diego and his pride were much too close for comfort, and Ford and Madison were tired. They could continue running through the jungle and hoping Diego wouldn't catch them, but their better option would be to hide. The problem was that Ford didn't know where one could hide in the jungle. He might have been able to if he could shift, but what about Madison?

"I can't believe you did this," Madison ranted as he ran. "You betrayed me, and I was stupid enough to believe everything you said."

"I didn't betray you," Ford said.

"Didn't you? Wasn't that your brother, the alpha of the lost pride? He said you told him you'd hand me over."

"Madison—"

There. Ford could hear the sound of water, which hopefully meant they'd be able to wash off their scent and interrupt their trail. They might even lose Diego and the pride if they stayed in the water for a bit.

The sound of water became stronger, too strong to just be a river. Ford gaped when he and Madison burst from between the trees to find himself standing in front of a waterfall. He heard Madison suck in a breath and wished he could kiss him here, in front of the waterfall.

He was pretty sure Madison would punch him in the face if he tried.

It was beautiful. The water fell from a rounded, tall rise of stone to end in a deep blue pond that was surrounded by trees and vegetation. Large round stones covered the ground, and the sun peeked above the waterfall, illuminating the scene.

There was no time, so Ford pulled Madison along. Madison squawked, but Ford couldn't let himself care. He knew Madison was angry and hurt, and he probably would never want to see Ford again once this was over, but that wasn't something they could deal with at the moment.

They slipped and stumbled their way to the waterfall. They were wet to the bones even before they reached it, but it didn't matter. They had to wade through the water, and Ford's pants clung to his legs as he and Madison disappeared in the darkness behind the water.

Ford didn't know what they'd find there, but the ledge of stone they were on was big enough for them to huddle behind the water. There was no way Diego and his pride would be able to smell them here, and hopefully, they wouldn't realize that was where they were hiding. They'd be safe if they could stay here until the pride gave up.

As soon as they stopped, Madison snatched his hand away from Ford and turned on him.

"Tell me the truth," he demanded.

"I never meant to hurt you," Ford whispered.

"Well, you failed. I'm hurt. I'm also pissed, and I want answers."

Ford closed his eyes and leaned the back of his head against the cool stone behind him. "Diego is my half-brother. I grew up here with him until I was eight when my mother took me back to the States. That's where I spent most of my life, but I decided to come back a few years ago. There was nothing for me there."

"But here, you had your pride."

"Not my pride. They don't want me, and I don't want them."

"The alpha is your brother, which means that your father was the alpha before him. You were a pride member then, weren't you?"

Ford could only nod because Madison was right. "Diego always said he wanted me to come back, but even though I was a pride member before, I don't belong with them. No matter what my father and brother want to believe, I don't think I ever did."

"Are you sure?"

There was so much pain in Madison's voice. Ford reached for him, but Madison didn't allow him to touch him. It made sense, even though it hurt. Ford had betrayed Madison, and Madison wouldn't make things easy on him. Ford wouldn't have wanted him to, anyway.

"Before I got to know you, I was only in this for the money. I don't care about the temple, and I'm still not sure I believe in the magic it's supposed to have. I thought I'd guide you through the jungle for a few days and that you'd get bored and want to go back."

Madison snorted. "That didn't work."

"I was angry when I realized my brother had sent people after you. After I had to fight that jaguar, I called Diego. I was scared both for you and me, and I didn't want either of us to get hurt. I told Diego that I'd bring you to him as long as he promised he wouldn't hurt you."

"And you believed him?"

"I don't know. I think I had to. I didn't want to see you hurt."

Ford reached for Madison, but Madison batted his hand away. "Don't touch me or try to convince me that you did this for me. You didn't. You did it for you and for what you'd gain, and that's all." He licked his lips. "Was telling me you care about me part of the plan? Were you trying to make me trust you even more? Was all of that a lie, too?"

"It wasn't," Ford promised. "I truly do care about you, and I'd already changed my mind when we got into town. I called Diego and told him I wouldn't hand you over. I didn't want to tell him why you were trying to get to the temple, but maybe I should have."

Ford reached for Madison again, but Madison wouldn't let him touch him. "Stop this," he hissed. "Stay away from me." He moved closer to the waterfall's edge as if he was about to run.

"You can't go." Ford panicked at the thought of Diego catching Madison. What would he do to him? Ford hadn't cared before, even though he hadn't wanted to see Madison hurt, but now, it felt like his world was crumbling down around him. He needed Madison to be okay, and he didn't know what Diego had in mind.

Madison shook his head. "I also can't stay here. I don't want to see you ever again. You betrayed me."

Ford hated that Madison was right—he *had* betrayed him—and didn't know what to do to fix this.

He wasn't sure there *was* anything he could do to fix it.

CHAPTER THIRTEEN

The trudge back through the jungle had been miserable. Madison hadn't been able to ditch Ford because he'd have gotten lost if he had, but they hadn't spoken the entire time it had taken them to reach Ford's car. It had gone faster because they hadn't been looking for anything, but it had still been two days Madison could have done without. Ford had tried talking to him, but Madison had ignored him. His betrayal had hurt, and it still did.

But Madison had found the temple, and in the end, that was what mattered.

What mattered even more was that he needed to find Ashley. He still had no idea what had happened to her and wasn't leaving this place without her. The problem was that she hadn't been at the temple, so where was she? Was she even alive?

Madison stared at the ceiling of his hotel room and tried to find a solution. As soon as they'd reached the city, he'd left Ford. He'd been hiding in Ashley's hotel room for two days, and he still wasn't close to knowing where she was. Ford had tried calling him, or at least Madison assumed it was him. He hadn't recognized the number, so he hadn't answered.

It hadn't been easy to resist the urge. It could have been the person who had Ashley, and that was someone Madison wanted to talk to. He hadn't wanted to risk it, but now, he was regretting it. Maybe he could have answered and hung up if it had been Ford.

His heart broke every time he thought of the man. He'd

truly believed they had something, and maybe they did. Madison couldn't trust him anymore, though, which meant that what they had didn't matter.

He grabbed the second pillow and pressed it against his face, screaming into it. It was childish, but it helped with the pain that had clung to his chest since he'd found out what Ford had done. Madison wanted to rage at him, hit him, and tell him he hated him, but he could do none of those things.

For one, he didn't hate Ford. He couldn't, not when he'd already fallen in love with him. He was lucky he hadn't told Ford. The man would have probably laughed in his face or something.

But even as he thought that, Madison couldn't stop thinking about the face Ford had made when the alpha had told Madison the truth. He'd been panicked, and he'd scrambled to make sure Madison knew he cared. Maybe he'd only been in this for the money, or maybe there had been something more. Madison didn't know, and he wouldn't find out.

It was over — at least the thing with Ford. Madison wasn't leaving this place without Ashley, though, which meant he needed to find her.

He threw the pillow at the foot of the bed and sat up. His phone was on the mattress next to him, and he snatched it up, unlocked it, and opened the browser. He poked around the Internet for a bit, but googling *how to find the alpha of the lost pride* wasn't helping. He bit his lower lip and decided to look into Ford. The alpha was his brother, so maybe he'd be able to find him through Ford.

It took too much digging into Ford's social media to find his brother. The alpha's profile was private, but the picture didn't lie. His dark eyes looked out at Madison from the phone, making him shiver. The man was very clearly an alpha, and Madison realized how lucky he'd been to come out of the temple in one piece. Maybe what he was about to do was foolish, and maybe he'd regret it, but he'd regret not trying even more. He owed it to Ashley to help her, even if it meant putting himself in danger. She'd found the temple, and that was what mattered, even though he hadn't been allowed to use its magic. Even more so, she was his friend, and no one deserved to vanish in the jungle the way she had.

Through Diego's profile, Madison found the website of his construction company. There was a phone number, and he clicked on it, his heart racing. He could do this. He could talk to the alpha, tell him he wanted Ashley back, and promise they would leave the country as soon as she was free. Hopefully, that would be enough to let them both go.

"LP construction company, how can I help you?" a perky woman asked.

Madison cleared his throat. "I need to talk to Diego." He didn't know if the woman was human or a pride member, and he wasn't going to risk it. The last thing he needed was to out the pride without the alpha's permission.

"Can I ask who's calling?"

"My name is Madison Williams. It's about his brother, Ford." It wasn't about Ford, but maybe it would get Diego to answer.

"One moment, please."

Madison could hear her talk to someone in the background, and after a moment, he was transferred to another phone. He held his breath until he heard Diego's voice. He didn't think he'd ever forget it after the temple.

"Hello?" Diego asked.

"My name is Madison Williams. We met a few days ago in the temple."

"You're Ford's boyfriend."

Madison snorted. "Definitely not. I paid him to get me through the jungle and to the temple. That's all there was to it."

"If you're sure," Diego drawled.

He was almost as infuriating as Ford, and Madison could see the family resemblance. He wanted to strangle Diego, too, but he forced himself to forget about it. "I need to talk to you about my friend."

"What friend?"

"She's the one who found the temple. She sent me an email with pictures, which is how I'm sure of it. She was kidnapped, and I'm not going anywhere without her. If you let her go, I promise we'll both get on the first plane and go home. You'll never hear from us again, and we won't mention the temple or the lost pride."

"Do you know anything about what happened to her? Ford mentioned her before, but he didn't know much."

It was an odd question, but Madison went along with it. "Nothing except that someone searched her hotel room."

"I see. How can I believe that you'll truly leave the country without trying to find the temple again or that you won't return?"

"I suppose you can only take my word for it. Ashley and I are both historians. We want the world to know about the temple, but it belongs to the lost pride. That's more important than anything else, and if you don't want anyone to know about it, we'll respect that. You can look us up if you want to make sure we're legit. Besides, most people don't believe in the lost pride and its temple. Even if we were to tell someone, they wouldn't believe us without proof, and we don't have any."

"You just said you had an email with pictures."

"They could be from anywhere in the world."

"I see."

"I promise we'll stay away if you let both of us go free."

"Why don't you come to pride territory?"

That sounded like a trap, but what was Madison supposed

to do? "Did you kill her? Are you planning on killing me, too?"

To his surprise, Diego laughed. "We haven't killed anyone. I'll send you instructions so you can reach us. I swear that no one will touch either you or your friend. You'll be safe, and we'll allow you to leave pride territory anytime you want."

Madison didn't have a choice. "All right. I'll come."

The only reason Ford grabbed his phone when it rang was that he hoped it was Madison. Instead, Diego's name was on the screen, and he almost didn't answer. He knew better than to ignore his brother, though. Diego would send someone to find him, and that was the last thing Ford wanted.

What he did want was to be left alone so he could lick his wounds and mope. He'd lost the only person he'd ever fallen in love with, and his heart didn't know how to deal with that. He'd tried calling Madison a few times but hadn't been surprised when Madison hadn't answered. He'd been clear that he wanted nothing to do with Ford ever again, and no matter how much it hurt, Ford needed to respect that.

He just wanted to know that Madison was okay. Maybe he was already on a plane back home, but something told Ford that wasn't so. Knowing Madison, he wouldn't give up on finding his friend, which meant he might get himself in trouble again. That was why Ford had called, or at least, it was what he told himself. He *hadn't* been about to grovel and beg Madison to take him back.

"What do you want?" he answered.

"Hello to you, too," Diego said. He sounded amused, which made Ford angry.

"I don't want to talk to you or anyone from your pride ever again. In fact, I'm thinking about moving back to the States."

There was a pause, and Ford regretted his words for a

second. He didn't want to hurt Diego. He might have told Madison what Ford had done, but in the end, all of this had been Ford's fault, and he needed to accept that.

"Your friend is coming over to pride territory," Diego said.

Ford pushed up from his bed. "What are you talking about?"

"He somehow managed to find me through the construction company. He called and said he wanted his friend back."

"You have her?"

Diego snorted. "You know, all of this would have been easier if you'd just talked to me."

"How was I supposed to do that? Your people were shooting at me, remember?"

"No, they weren't."

"Don't start lying. You've never been a liar, and it's one of the few things I've always liked about you."

"It's good to know there's something you like about me, but I promise I'm not lying. Those weren't my people, at least not in the way you think."

"What are you talking about?"

"You know some groups in the pride are more traditional. They want us to go back to being in the jungle, away from humans, but most of the pride disagrees. They're fine with the way we are now, and they don't want to lose the commodities of living with humans."

"I don't care about any of that. What will you do to Madison?"

"Nothing. He wants his friend back, and I'll make sure they're allowed to leave without anyone trying to stop them. Why don't you come over? That way, you can keep an eye on me and make sure I don't hurt your friend."

It was so tempting to say yes, even though Madison wouldn't be happy. He didn't want Madison to get hurt, but he also didn't want him to hate him any more than he already did. "I don't think it's a good idea."

Diego made a surprised sound. "Why not?"

"Because he hates me and told me he never wants to see me again."

"So you're going to stay away?"

"I don't have a choice."

"You really care about him, don't you?"

Ford almost denied it, but what was the point? He did care about Madison. He'd fallen half in love with the professor one day into their trip in the jungle, and after the night they'd spent together at the hotel, he'd crossed the line into loving him fully. That was why he needed to stay away. "I love him."

"That's not something I ever expected to hear from you."

"It's not something I ever expected to feel, but here we are. Please keep him safe."

"I will, but I think you should come. I want you to know the truth, and I'd rather tell both of you at the same time."

That was the only excuse Ford needed. He wanted to do what Madison wished for, but he'd probably never see him again after today. It would hurt like hell, and while Ford wondered why he was willing to torture himself like that, he didn't care about the answer. "Fine. I'm coming. You better make sure no one bothers him, because if they do, I won't hesitate to beat them up."

Diego laughed. "There's the Ford I know. You never give up, even when the odds are against you."

Ford hung up without answering and jumped off his bed. Diego was right. He had a hard time giving up when he wanted something, and this was one of the occasions in which he shouldn't. Madison might hate him, but hate was so very close to love. They were both strong feelings that made it almost impossible to stay away from the person one felt them for. Madison might hate Ford, but he might also love him, and that was all Ford needed.

That and a chance to grovel and beg Madison to take him back.

Chapter Fourteen

Ford remembered pride territory from childhood, but he'd never come back after his mother had taken him away. Even after moving back to the area, he knew he didn't belong in pride territory. He found his way there easily, though, and parked his car in front of the house that once belonged to his father.

He gripped the steering wheel, uneasy with what was about to happen. He didn't like the feeling of bothering Madison and not giving him what he needed, but he was in love for the first time. He wasn't giving up that easily, even though he'd been the one to fuck it up.

Madison was far from perfect. He was hyper-focused, clumsy, and loud. He was also the man Ford had fallen in love with against all odds. That was enough for Ford to want to be here, so he took a deep breath and climbed out of his car.

He ignored the stares. It was either that or flipping off everyone staring, which didn't feel like the best idea. He wasn't here to start a fight, to ask his brother to become a pride member, or to spend time with him. He was here for Madison, and as soon as Madison had what he needed, he and Ford would get out of pride territory and never come back.

The place hadn't changed much since Ford was a child. It looked like a small town, with Diego's house in the middle of it on the tiny main street. Pride territory was gathered around it, mostly made up of other houses, although there were a few stores. The pride traveled to the nearest city for most of the things they needed, but they had the essentials, and they'd always seemed happy. Ford had spent his childhood playing with other kids, climbing trees, and being free. He'd felt like he belonged then, but now, nothing could be further from the truth. He didn't know this place anymore, and these people didn't know or want him here.

He raised his chin high and ignored them. He quickly reached his brother's door and knocked. Ford wanted to explain why Madison had been seeking out the temple, and he hoped Diego would listen to him and give Madison a chance. No one deserved it more than him.

The door swung open. Diego looked almost happy to see Ford, which Ford didn't understand. "Is he already here?" he asked.

"Not yet. You're early."

"It's on purpose. Can I come in?"

"Of course." Diego's expression softened, and he smiled. "Dad would be happy to have both of us here."

Ford's heart broke a little at the thought of his father. Ford's mother had never let him come back after they'd left the country, and when Ford was sixteen, his father had died without Ford being allowed to see him again. It was one of the reasons Ford didn't talk to his mother anymore. She'd taken a lot from him, and while he understood why she'd done so, it was only in part. She'd felt isolated and like she didn't belong, but that hadn't been the case for Ford. Even if she'd wanted to leave, she could have allowed him to visit regularly. Instead, she'd taken Ford away from the only home and family he'd had, and he'd never get them back.

He walked in, not surprised to see that the house had changed. It was more modern, but still cozy and a place Ford could easily call home. That was what he'd done for the first eight years of his life, but there were no signs of the child Ford had been here. His mother had made sure of that.

Ford wished he could go deeper inside the house, explore

it, and see how many things had changed, but instead, he stood up tall and faced his brother. "I need to tell you why Madison was looking for the temple."

Diego blinked. "Because he's a historian."

So Diego *had* talked to Madison. "In part, yes." Ford hated to break Madison's confidence, but it was the only way to give him a chance to get what he needed. "But there's a deeper reason. Hell, it's the reason why he became a historian, to begin with." Ford licked his lips. "He knows about the legends."

"Many people do."

"Yes, but he believes them. He was very close to his grandmother. From what he told me, she pretty much raised him, and she's the reason he loves history as much as he does. She believed in the legends, and she transferred her passion to him. She died a few years ago, and he wants her back. He was never going to steal anything from the temple, but he hoped to use its magic to get his grandmother back. I'm sure that if you ask him to keep the temple and its location secret, he will."

"Knowing that helps explain why he's here, but I'm not sure why you're telling me this. What do you want me to do?"

"Give him a chance. I know you don't owe him anything, but he's not the one asking. I am. You always say I'm your brother and that you care about me, so please, give me this. I won't even hold the fact that you sent people to shoot at us against you." Ford felt he needed to offer more. He swallowed, knowing he might regret this, but it wasn't enough to stop him. "I'll become a pride member."

Diego was silent for a moment. He was staring, and Ford avoided looking back at him. He didn't think he could take it.

"You'd be willing to become a pride member if I do this for Madison?" Diego finally asked.

"I am."

"Why? You always say no when I ask you to become a pride member. Clearly, you don't want it, yet you're here, telling me you'll do it."

"Because I love him, all right?" Ford raked a hand through his hair and stepped away. "I know it's ridiculous. I've known him for such a short time that it shouldn't be possible, and he's going back to his life in the US. He probably won't ever think about me again, but I don't care about any of that. I know how much losing his grandmother hurts him. If there's any chance he could get her back, I want to give him that. I'd do pretty much anything to make it happen, including becoming one of your pride members."

Ford turned toward his brother, but the front door opened before Diego could say anything. Ford blinked, wondering who was there. For a moment, he thought it was someone familiar with Diego, which would explain why they'd opened the door without knocking, but the person on the other side wasn't there for Diego.

Madison stared at Ford with wide eyes from the doorstep, and Ford was pretty sure he'd heard everything he'd just confessed to his brother.

Madison hadn't meant to hear what Ford was telling his brother. He'd just reached pride territory, had found Diego's house, and had been ready to knock on the door. That was when he'd heard the sound of two men talking, and he'd decided not to knock just yet to give them a chance to finish the conversation.

He hadn't realized it was Ford until Ford's voice had become loud enough that Madison could hear what he was saying. After Ford confessed he loved Madison and that he'd sacrifice pretty much anything to make him happy, Madison couldn't stay away. He'd pushed open the door, even though it wasn't his place to do so. He didn't know how the alpha would react, but he didn't care. He just needed to see Ford.

And now, he was seeing him. Ford stood in front of the alpha, but he wasn't looking at him. Instead, he was staring at Madison with his mouth slightly open. Madison was pretty sure his expression was similar. He was in shock and didn't know how to react.

Of course, he'd known he was in love with Ford, but he hadn't believed Ford felt the same. He'd expected him only to have been in this for the money, especially after what had happened in the temple. He hadn't expected to find Ford here, and he certainly hadn't expected to hear him confess all of this.

"Mr. Williams?" Diego asked, breaking the spell.

Madison blinked and turned his attention to the alpha. "Madison, please."

Diego smiled. Madison had seen he was handsome back at the temple, but he'd been terrified and freaking out. It had also been fairly dark, but now that the two brothers stood in front of him, he could see the family resemblance.

Madison did his best not to look at Ford. He was here for Ashley, and while he wanted nothing more than to throw himself at Ford, knowing she was safe was more important.

"And you can call me Diego," the alpha said. "You're important to my brother, which means you're important to me."

So they weren't going to ignore what Madison had heard. "I just want my friend back. Is she all right?"

Diego's smile widened. "She is. Why don't the two of you come with me?"

Madison was pretty sure Diego wouldn't hurt them. He'd been scared back at the temple, but now, he doubted Diego would do anything to him. The alpha was just trying to protect his pride, and Madison could understand that.

He nodded. "Are you taking me to Ashley?"

"Eventually. I'd also like to explain everything to both of you. Ford knows a bit about the situation, but you don't, and I don't want you thinking that I've been hunting you through the jungle."

Madison frowned. "Those were your men shooting at us, weren't they?"

"They were."

Diego gestured at the door, and Madison took a step back to allow him and Ford to step through. He and Ford glanced at each other, and Madison had to resist the urge to throw himself into his arms.

He didn't know if he'd forgiven Ford. Back at the temple, he'd felt betrayed, and he still did, but being away from Ford had allowed him to think about what had happened. He and Ford hadn't known each other initially. It made sense that Ford had agreed to hand him over for the money. When he'd started caring for Madison, he'd been scared at the thought of telling him the truth, as anyone would have been. He'd known Madison wouldn't take it well, and if Diego hadn't been at the temple, Ford would never have had to tell Madison he'd been planning to hand him over and had then changed his mind. It would have been easier, and Madison could understand why Ford would have wanted that, even though he didn't agree with the decision.

"As I started to explain to my brother earlier, some of my pride members are much more traditional than me," Diego said as they walked through the village.

Madison was in awe and dying to ask questions about the lost pride and their territory, but he didn't dare. Maybe later he'd have time to. He'd believed he and Ashley would be chased out of here, but now that he was talking to Diego, he didn't think so.

"Some of them want us to go back to the jungle. They want the lost pride to stay lost, and I understand why they feel that way. It doesn't mean it's the best thing for the pride, or that I agree. I'm the alpha, which means that what I decide is the law. Unfortunately, a few of my pride members decided to take things into their own hands. They wanted you and your friend to stay away from the temple and were ready to do anything to make sure you did. They shot at you when you first entered the jungle and fought with Ford, but they weren't the ones who tried picking you up at the hotel. Those were my people, and they wouldn't have hurt you."

"You mean part of your pride went rogue?" Ford asked.

"They did. I've already punished them, and they won't touch Madison ever again. They also won't try to hurt you. I'm sorry all of this happened, but I never meant for anyone to get hurt. I did want Madison to stay away from the temple, but I would never have hurt him to make it so. The lost pride has always guarded the temple, but we were more open about it, and I feel that maybe we need to be again."

"What do you mean?" Madison was afraid to hope, so he told himself there was no way it meant what he thought.

Diego flashed him a smile. "The temple used to be open to the people who needed it. There was a vetting process, but most people were welcome. It hasn't been that way in hundreds of years, and while I understand why people feel the temple belongs to the pride, I feel like part of it belongs to the world, too. Is it fair for us to keep it to ourselves?"

"Yes," Madison blurted out. "Because if you made it public knowledge, people would start coming from all over the world, including governments. Things aren't the way they were back when the temple was built. They're much more complicated now, and I think it would be a mistake for you to open the temple that way."

Diego cocked his head. "I can't say I expected you to say that."

"I didn't expect to feel this way, but this place is precious.

I don't want the temple or the pride to be destroyed by greediness."

"Which is why I'm taking you there."

They'd entered the jungle, and Madison hadn't understood why, but he'd been focused on Diego, so he hadn't wondered too much. Now, he did. "Why?"

"Because you're right. We both are. The pride needs to find a way to open the temple to the people who deserve it without gathering too much attention. I don't know how we'll make it work, but maybe you can help us. And maybe you can be the first person in recent years to benefit from the magic present in the temple."

Madison gasped when he realized what Diego was saying. He hadn't allowed himself to hope, but maybe he should have.

"We don't have anything for the trek in the jungle," he tried.

"Then it's good that the temple is much closer to pride territory than you'd expect."

It was. Madison hadn't realized it before, mostly because he still wasn't entirely sure where the temple was. He and Ford had stumbled onto it but hadn't taken down the coordinates. They hadn't had time, and after they'd started walking back to Ford's car, Madison hadn't wanted to. He didn't want anyone to be able to find it, including himself.

But now, cutting through pride territory, he could already see the first stone walls. This side of the temple was much cleaner, including the pathway that led to it. Clearly, the pride still took care of the place, which Madison liked.

"Our duty has always been to protect the temple and take care of it and its magic," Diego said, his voice going softer as they neared the back entrance. "Things aren't exactly the way they were before, but we've been doing our job. The temple is intact, and the magic is waiting for you."

Madison hesitated at the entrance. "Are you sure? Because you don't have to do this for me. I understand this place belongs to your pride."

"And it's because of that that I offer you this. You seem like a good person, Madison, and the fact that my brother likes you makes me like you, too. I need you to think about what you're about to do, though. Bringing people back from death isn't always the right thing to do. Actually, it often isn't. Is this what your grandmother would have wanted? Are you doing this for her, or are you doing it for you?"

Madison licked his lips. He understood what Diego was saying, but he was so close. "How does it work?"

Diego didn't go in. Instead, he gestured at Madison to do so. "The magic will take care of everything. Just walk in, go to the altar, and focus on what you want."

Madison was scared. He hadn't thought he would be, but it made his chest feel tight. Fear wouldn't be enough to stop him. He wanted this so much he could taste it, and he was finally close enough to grab it. The magic was real, and his grandmother was coming back.

Sucking in a breath, he stepped through the entrance.

Ford couldn't believe what his brother had just done. He hadn't expected it and wasn't sure how to thank Diego or what Diego would want as payment. What if Diego demanded that he become a pride member?

He'd do it. He'd do pretty much anything for Madison, something that still bewildered him. He didn't know how to deal with those feelings or how to feel about the fact that he had them, but right now, none of that mattered. The only thing that did was Madison, and Ford wanted to be there for him.

He took a step forward to join him inside the temple.

Diego's hand shot out, stopping Ford from doing so. When Ford looked at him, ready to fight, he shook his head.

"This is something he has to do on his own."

"Is it safe? What if something happens to him?" And Ford was outside, unable to help him?

Diego cocked his head and stared at him. "I have a hard time believing how much you care about him."

Ford snorted. "Believe me. You're not the only one. I just don't want anything to happen to him."

"Nothing will happen. I know the temple's magic, Ford. Every pride member does. It'll do what it does best, which is healing people in whatever way they need to be healed. If there's someone who deserves it, it's your Madison."

Ford couldn't stop himself from smiling. "He does. He's a good person, and he'll make sure no one finds out where the temple is. He doesn't want to create trouble for your pride. He just wants someone he loves back."

"I think everyone can understand that. I'm sorry about what happened. If I'd known my people had gotten out of hand, I would have stepped in sooner."

Ford nodded, and while he cared about his brother, he was more interested in what was happening in the temple. He wondered what would have happened if he'd gone straight to his brother when Madison had mentioned the temple. Diego would no doubt have stepped in, and Madison probably never would have been in the temple. Ford wouldn't have gotten to know him, and he wouldn't have fallen in love with him.

A gasp made Ford move toward the entrance again, but Diego shook his head. It was enough to stop Ford from going in, even though Diego wasn't his alpha. It was hard, and his entire body vibrated with the need to be close to Madison and make sure he was all right.

The sound of soft padding of feet made Ford perk up. He

stared at the entrance, waiting for Madison to come out.

Madison might want some alone time with his grandmother, and Ford didn't want to intrude, but he was worried.

Ford shouldn't have been. When Madison appeared, he was in his wolf form. Ford didn't know how long it usually took him to shift, but he'd made it sound like it would have taken longer than the time he'd spent in the temple.

Ford stared at him with wide eyes before peeking behind him. Was his grandmother there? It sounded too good to be true to have a relic that could bring people back from the dead, but if Diego said it worked, then, it did. Ford should have had more faith, but he was starting to realize that he should have had more faith in many things.

He glanced at Diego, who nodded. Ford was cautious as he approached Madison in case Madison was still angry at him. He wouldn't blame him if that was the case. Considering what he'd done, Ford expected Madison not to want him in his life anymore, and while he didn't like it, he wouldn't argue.

Not too much, anyway.

Madison stopped in front of Ford. Ford crouched and held out a hand, unsure how to behave. It wasn't that Madison was a wolf shifter, but rather that there were no signs of his grandmother, and she was why he was here. Ford had no idea what had happened in the temple and why she was nowhere to be seen. What if it hadn't worked?

Madison was a gorgeous human, but he was also a gorgeous wolf. His fur ranged from white to black, with various shades of gray in between. His muzzle was white, but the tip of his tail was black. His blue eyes were soft and fringed by long lashes, and as Ford stared at him, one of his ears flicked.

Ford curled his fingers. "You're beautiful," he murmured.

He didn't expect Madison to bump his muzzle against his fingers, but he was elated when he did. It was almost as if

Madison was forgiving him, which he didn't deserve. If Madison wanted to be petted, Ford was happy to give him that.

He stroked his fingertips on top of Madison's head. Madison made a rumbling noise and pressed closer, almost pushing Ford onto his ass. Ford laughed and grabbed onto Madison, who gave him a toothy grin.

"I don't expect you to become a pride member for this," Diego said.

He was looking at Ford and Madison, and at that moment, Ford would have said yes to pretty much anything his brother might ask. "I thought it was what you wanted," Ford pointed out as he stroked Madison's soft fur.

Diego's smile was wistful. "I do wish you didn't see me as a stranger, but I understand why you do. I just want us to be close and rebuild our relationship. We missed out on too much, but we didn't have a choice. Now that we do, it would be great to be real brothers again."

Ford didn't know what to say, so he just nodded. Thankfully, Madison distracted both of them by shifting back to his human form. He sat on the ground, blinking, for a moment. He was naked, but Ford and Diego were shifters, too, and they were used to it. It usually didn't bother shifters, but Madison's cheeks suddenly flushed with awareness.

Ford wanted to ask what had happened. Madison's grandmother wasn't here, and he'd shifted back much faster than Ford had expected.

Madison jumped to his feet and rushed into the temple. Ford laughed, even though he was confused. Madison hadn't seemed angry or sad, just embarrassed.

Madison came out of the temple minutes later, his shirt still unbuttoned. He'd put on his pants and shoes, though, and he launched himself at Ford. They hugged for a moment that didn't feel nearly long enough before Madison pushed away to hug Diego, too. That hug was much shorter, and Madison turned to Ford again seconds later, wrapping his arms around him a second time.

"I understand what you were saying earlier now," Madison said. "I wanted my grandmother back because I felt that I didn't have anyone else in the world who would love me the way she did. I thought I was alone without her, but I was wrong."

Diego smiled. "You talked to her."

"I did. She was happy to see me and to find out that I'd fallen in love. We talked, and when I told her what I was trying to do, she refused. She doesn't feel she belongs anymore, and I don't think she's wrong. She's lived her life, and now it's time for me to live mine. She made it easier for me by using the magic to help me with my shift." Madison looked up at Ford. "I never shifted that easily before."

"You looked good," Ford said, reassuring him.

Madison couldn't stop smiling, even when he turned back to Diego. "I swear I'll keep the secret. I don't want the world to ruin the pride and the temple. The pride is the guardian of the magic, and I trust it to make the right decisions when it comes to allowing people to visit."

Diego nodded. "Thank you. If you leave me your contact info, I'll make sure to let you know what's happening. And of course, you're always welcome to visit."

Madison's eyes lit up at the same time as Ford's heart broke.

It looked like Madison was going to say yes to visiting, and Ford didn't blame him, but how could he survive knowing Madison was here? He'd just told Diego he would give him anything he wanted to help Madison, and Diego wished for their relationship to be stronger. That meant spending time with the pride, and it sounded like Madison would, too. They'd have to see each other, which wouldn't be easy.

"I'd love to have the opportunity to study the temple.

Ashley and I both would," Madison said.

Diego's smile widened. "Come. I'll take you to your friend."

Madison shot Ford an uncertain glance, but Ford shrugged because he had no idea what was happening. He trusted his brother, so the two of them followed Diego back to the area where the pride lived.

Ford's thoughts swirled. He didn't know how he'd deal with what came next, but he couldn't deny Madison any of this. Madison would be able to study the temple for as long as he wanted. It was his life's dream come true, and Ford wouldn't take that away from him, no matter how much it cost him.

"For a while after you told me about your friend, I wasn't sure who you were talking about," Diego explained. "I didn't have anyone kidnapped, and when I interrogated the members of the pride who went rogue, they swore they didn't kidnap anyone, either. They did raid a hotel room looking for information, but they said that was all they did."

"But it doesn't make sense," Madison said. "Ashley just vanished. I haven't been able to call her, and I have no idea where she is. Her room was ransacked."

"They were lying. I had my people search every building in town, and they found her. She's been freed, but I'm not sure she's happy about that."

Madison sucked in a breath. "I'm sorry?"

"One of my pride members came to me a few days ago. He told me he'd fallen in love with her and that he wanted to bring her into the pride. I thought it was fast, but who am I to judge? She wants to stay and become part of the pride, and I'm inclined to say yes."

Madison was silent for so long that Ford wondered what he was thinking. He wasn't surprised when eventually, Madison swore.

"I'm going to strangle her," he said, stomping ahead as if he knew where to find her. "She's been free long enough to fall in love, but she didn't think to call me?"

Diego laughed. "I'd rather you not hurt her, since she's one of my pride members."

"She let me believe something bad happened to her long after she was saved. If it weren't for that damn email and for the fact that she wasn't answering her phone, I wouldn't be here."

"And you wouldn't have talked to your grandmother again," Ford pointed out.

Madison glared, but it quickly turned into a smile again. "And I wouldn't have met you," he whispered.

Ford's heart raced. Maybe not everything was lost, after all.

Chapter Fifteen

Madison couldn't believe what had happened over the past week. It had been a whirlwind of activity, and it had left his mind reeling. He still couldn't wrap it around everything, but he was starting to settle, which was good, considering he was headed home.

Ashley was okay. She'd been sheepish when Madison finally found her, had apologized at least once a day since then, and had told him she wasn't returning to the US. Diego hadn't been lying when he'd said she was a pride member now. She'd fallen in love with one of Diego's people, and Diego had given her the opportunity of a lifetime. She'd be able to study the temple and its magic, which was all she'd ever wanted.

Well, along with the hunk she now called her boyfriend.

Madison hoped everything worked out for her. He wanted her to be happy, and he'd been able to see that being with the pride and studying the temple was what she needed to feel that way. He wished he could stay, too, but he'd already been here too long. His mother had started calling him daily to ask when he was returning, and the university had also reached out. He'd been gone for longer than he'd expected, and they weren't happy with him. He'd explained it had been an emergency, so they'd given him a bit of leeway, but it was time for him to go.

He looked around the hotel room he'd taken over. Ashley had come back with him a few days ago to get her stuff, so it was neat now. All of Madison's things were packed into his bags, and he was ready to go to the airport.

He was going to miss this place. He wouldn't miss running through the jungle while being shot at, or the mosquitoes, but the temple and the pride had given him what he'd wanted for most of his life.

And he wasn't only thinking about talking to his grand-mother one last time and the gift she'd given him.

It was incredible, and he'd been shifting more often than necessary since that first time. Everyone indulged him, even though they couldn't understand how it felt. They didn't know what Madison had been through because of his diffi-culties to shift, but Madison was glad for it. He'd been an odd-ity and never wanted anyone to go through that.

A knock on the door made him turn. He sucked in a breath and went to open, knowing his time here was over. Ford was giving him a ride to the airport, and that was probably the last time Madison would see him.

He swung open the door, smiling at the sight of Ford on the other side of it. They hadn't talked about what had hap-pened between them, but they needed to, and they didn't have much time left.

"Ready?" Ford asked.

Madison nodded and gestured at his luggage. He wasn't surprised when Ford stepped into the room to grab it, and he didn't protest. He already knew Ford would brush him off.

Madison was tempted to stay. Diego had offered him a place with the pride, and Madison wanted Ford more than ever. It felt like everything he yearned for was here, but his life was in the US.

Right?

His family was. His job was.

He just wasn't sure there was anything else for him there.

It would be good to be in a familiar place and to go back to a routine, but that was the only thing he was looking forward to. Oh, and showing his mother that he was finally the shifter she'd always wanted him to be. She'd be over the moon happy, but he already felt bitter about it. She loved him, but she would love him even more now that he was *normal*, which wasn't how things were supposed to work. He'd been a shifter all along, no matter how difficult it had been for him. His mother's love shouldn't change just because of something he hadn't been able to change.

He and Ford were silent as they left the hotel and climbed into Ford's car. Madison didn't know what to say, but he also didn't know what he wanted or how he felt. He and Ford had been awkward with each other since the temple, and Madison didn't like it. Yes, Ford had betrayed him, but was it so bad that Madison should stay away from him?

Madison was starting to feel it wasn't. Ford had been trying to save himself, which Madison could understand. People had been shooting at them, and Ford had been wounded. Anyone else in his place would have wanted to save their ass, and the best way for him to do that had been to hand Madison over. Ford knew his brother, so he'd been sure Diego wouldn't hurt Madison.

And as soon as he'd realized that what he felt for Madison was more than friendship, he'd changed his mind. Diego had confirmed that Ford had called to tell him he would no longer hand Madison over. Madison was glad Ford had felt that way and even more so that Ford had protected him. Things could have been wildly different if Ford hadn't changed his mind, and now that he'd had time to think about it, Madison understood. He wasn't angry anymore.

And he wasn't going to leave without telling Ford that.

"I'm sorry I have to go," he murmured.

"I'm sorry, too. We both knew it was going to happen, though."

"I guess. My life is there, after all."

Not a life he enjoyed. Madison was jealous of Ashley. She'd found love and had the best opportunity of her life. She'd be allowed to study the temple for years to come, while Madison would only be back for the summers. He wanted to live here, too. He wanted everything Ford and Diego were offering.

But maybe he was too scared to take it.

It was easier for him to go back to his normal life. He knew what would happen day by day, could make plans, and would feel more settled. It was hard to say no to his dreams, but also a relief because it meant he wouldn't have to worry.

He was choosing safety over what he truly wanted and was very much aware of that. He just wasn't sure he could take the massive step he needed to take to be happy.

"I'll miss you," Ford whispered.

"I doubt you'll miss me bitching in the jungle and falling on my face."

Ford shot Madison a glance. "I'll miss that, too. The jungle won't be the same without you."

Madison's heart ached.

He was pretty sure nothing would be the same without Ford, but he didn't know if he was strong enough to do what he needed to change things.

Ford had known Madison would be going back, so he hadn't been surprised when Madison had asked him to drive him to the airport. His heart broke then, and it was breaking now, sitting in the car next to him. Ford wanted to throw himself on his knees and beg Madison to stay, but he didn't. He had dignity, but more importantly, he didn't want Madison to feel bad about what he was doing.

Of course he was going home. That was where his family and job were, just like Ford's family and job were here. He wasn't sure he'd ever be able to leave them behind, and it wouldn't be fair of him to ask Madison to do so.

Even though he felt like he couldn't breathe when he

thought about the rest of his life without Madison.

It shouldn't be possible to fall in love so quickly, but that was what Ford had done. Spending time with Madison over the past week hadn't helped, and neither had Diego's allusions to both of them staying with the pride. Madison wasn't staying, and Ford couldn't leave. That meant they couldn't be together.

But at least something good was coming out of all of this. Ford was closer than ever to his brother, and while he wasn't a pride member yet, he was starting to think that maybe it wouldn't be awful to be one. Spending time there had given him a feeling of belonging again, and it wasn't something he wanted to lose.

He was already losing enough.

"Well, I won't miss the jungle," Madison said. "But I'll miss you."

Ford couldn't stand it anymore. He quickly parked the car on the side of the road, ignoring Madison's squeak of surprise. He turned the engine off and twisted in his seat to look at Madison, but he didn't dare reach for him. They'd barely touched since Madison had found out about Ford's betrayal, and Ford couldn't let him go without kissing him one last time, but he wouldn't force him.

"I'll miss you, too. I'll miss you more than I've ever missed anything or anyone, and I don't know how to deal with that. I'm sorry for what I did," he blurted out. "I realize I betrayed you, and even though I thought it was the best thing for both of us at the time, it's not an excuse. I don't know if you'll ever be able to forgive me, and I don't need you to, but I just wanted to tell you how much you matter to me. You changed my life, Madison, and you did so for the better. I'll always hate myself for hurting you and making you feel like you couldn't trust me."

Ford yelped when Madison threw himself into his arms.

Thankfully, they were in the car, so they couldn't fall far. Ford's back hit the door, but he didn't care. Madison scrambled into his lap and kissed him, and *that* was all he cared about.

Madison's hands were twisted in Ford's hair as if he was afraid that if he let go, Ford would move back. Ford had no intention of doing that. He hugged Madison close, kissing him with all he had. He could almost believe that if he kissed Madison hard enough, Madison would change his mind and stay.

But things didn't work that way.

Madison was panting when he stopped kissing Ford and pressed their foreheads together. "I hate having to make this choice," he whispered.

"I know." Ford kissed Madison's nose. "But you made the right decision. Have faith in yourself."

"Even though I'm leaving?"

"You going back to your life doesn't mean we can't find a way to be together. Long-distance relationships are a thing."

Madison drew back. He looked skeptical, which Ford understood. "There's long-distance, and there's seeing each other only a few times a year."

"Maybe it'll be enough to begin with. We can find our way to each other. I believe in us."

Madison smiled. "I believe in us, too. I want you, and I'll do everything I can to have you. If that means having a long-distance relationship, then we better start thinking about ways to make it happen."

They did. They talked the entire time Ford drove Madison to the airport. Then, after Madison had passed through to departures and Ford couldn't see him anymore, Madison called him. They continued talking until Madison climbed on the plane, and when they hung up, Ford had hope.

For now, it was enough.

EPILOGUE

Things had been odd for a few days after Madison had arrived home. He was back at work now, which helped, but his life had been flipped upside down.

The biggest change was his mother. Like he'd expected, she'd been stunned but incredibly happy after he'd shifted in front of her. She'd been behaving differently since then, calling him almost every day and even attempting to set him up with some of her friends' sons. It was as if now that he could shift as easily as every other shifter, he finally deserved to be part of the family and to have what she deemed a full life.

He hated it. No matter how good her intentions were, it hurt, and he wasn't ready to forgive her for what she'd done to him over the years.

But he regularly talked to his father and his sister, and things felt like they were settling down. The problem was that there was a massive hole in Madison's life, and he didn't know how to fill it, or even if he could. It was even worse than when he'd lost his grandmother, maybe because Ford was out there somewhere.

He and Ford talked every day. It was both good and bad because Madison yearned for more, but he couldn't have it. It was better than nothing, though, which was why they continued calling each other, but he was already counting the days until the next time he could visit. He wanted to spend time with Ford, to explore the temple, but he was thousands of miles away, and everything that had happened there felt like a dream.

"Sir?" one of his students asked.

Madison shook himself and smiled. "I apologize," he told the class. "I've been distracted since I came back."

"How's your friend?" the same student asked.

Madison had mentioned he was leaving for a bit to help a friend, but he hadn't gone into details. He was pleasantly surprised to see that his students had listened to him and wanted to know how things had gone. "She's perfectly fine. She met someone."

The students laughed. "Did she decide to stay there?" someone else asked.

"She has. I don't have to tell you how jealous I am. Not only has she landed a great guy, but she can also study the lost pride right where they used to live. It's an incredible opportunity."

"Do you think the temple is real?"

Madison leaned his hip against his desk. "I don't know. Does it matter?"

"We study history, not things that never existed."

Madison nodded. "But we might never find out whether the temple was real or not, yet it won't stop us from studying the lost pride. Do any of you think they're out there, hiding from humans?"

"I think they're hiding *with* humans," a voice said.

Madison stared. For a second, he could have sworn it was Ford's voice. It didn't make sense and was impossible, so he dismissed it. "So you believe the lost pride still exists?"

"I'm sure they do."

Madison finally found the person the voice belonged to. His eyes widened, and his mouth dropped open as he stared at Ford.

He looked out of place and incredibly casual. Clearly, he wasn't a student, but he was relaxed and leaning back in his chair.

The students could tell something was up because they started whispering and looking from Madison to Ford.

Madison cleared his throat. "I apologize, but I have to end the class early."

"Looks like your friend wasn't the only one who met a gorgeous guy in the jungle," a female student said, causing the others to laugh.

Madison ignored them. He couldn't look away from Ford, and Ford couldn't seem to look away from him. They continued staring at each other as the students packed up their things and left, the door closing softly behind the last of them.

Then Madison and Ford were alone.

Madison rushed away from his desk. He stumbled on one of the steps, catching himself on his hands. He heard Ford swear, but he didn't care. He needed to get to Ford, and he needed to do it now.

Ford was on his feet and coming toward Madison when Madison reached him. He opened his arms, and Madison threw himself between them, wrapping his around Ford like an octopus. Ford was really here, and Madison wasn't letting him go.

Never again. Never again did he want to be away from Ford. It wasn't fair to either of them, and he'd missed Ford so badly since he'd come back that he'd already started looking into moving permanently closer to him. He didn't know what he'd do for a living, but there was nothing worth staying away from him.

Madison didn't like his job, and at the moment, he didn't like his mother much, either. He'd miss his sister and father, but he could visit. He could feel his place wasn't here anymore, but he hadn't been sure he had a place with the pride.

Now, he was.

He and Ford kissed, and it was like coming home. It was fierce for the first few moments but eventually settled into something soft and sweet. Madison hadn't realized he needed it so badly, but as he clung to Ford, he knew he never wanted to let go.

"What are you doing here?" he asked.

Ford grinned. "I missed you and decided to visit." His smile softened. "I realized how important you are to me. I don't want us to have a long-distance relationship. I want us to have a relationship, period, so I decided to come and see what happened."

Madison shook his head. "You're not staying."

"I am as long as you are. Your job is here."

"It is, and so is my family, but that doesn't matter. I have a family and a job in the jungle, too, and I have every intention of going back. Your brother offered me a place as a pride member and the opportunity to study the temple, and that's what I want to do. I don't know if it'll be enough for me to survive, but I'll find a way."

"Didn't Diego tell you he was willing to pay you to study the temple? Because he's paying your friend."

Madison made a strangled sound. "I'm going to yell at him when I next see him." He grinned. "I'm done resisting this, Ford. I want the temple, and I want you."

Ford kissed him again. "Then it's a good thing I want you, too. Come home, Madison."

Madison was going to.

Ford hadn't known what to expect when he'd decided to do this. He'd suspected that Madison wanted to stay with him, but it had been easier to go back. Here, his life was in order. He had a job, his family, and everything he'd known all his life. Back in the jungle, he'd have to get used to new people, a new setting, and new situations.

But new didn't mean bad. Ford would be there to support

Madison through all of it, and he couldn't wait. He wanted them to be together, and while he'd known that before Madison even left, he was even more sure now. The time they'd been apart had reinforced his certainty of how he felt about Madison, and it was time for them to start a life together.

He didn't know what that would look like, but as long as Madison was there, he didn't care. They'd work things out and find a way to be happy together.

Madison looked up at Ford, his eyes still wide. Ford wanted to wake up to him every day for the rest of his life, and he held his breath as he waited for Madison's answer.

"So your brother is offering me a job?" Madison asked.

It wasn't what Ford had wanted to hear, but it was a step forward. "I yelled at him when I realized he hadn't been clear about that. Yes, he wants to offer you a paid job. He and the pride have protected the temple for hundreds of years, but they don't know that much about it or the lost pride. Diego feels it's important that they find out more, and he's wondering if it would be possible to use the other ruins to attract tourists and visitors."

"There are other ruins?"

"Yeah. We used to play there when we were kids."

Madison playfully slapped Ford's shoulder. "Why didn't you tell me? I only got to look at the temple."

"I didn't think about it. Besides, I feel the temple was more than enough for the time you were there."

"Maybe, but I want to see all of it."

"If you say yes, you'll be able to. It's a lot of work, and only two of you will be doing it, but Diego feels it's the best way to go about this."

"But? Because I feel there's a *but*."

Ford cleared his throat. "Diego would feel more comfortable if the people studying the ruins and the lost pride were pride members. Your friend already is, of course, so she's not a problem."

"So I have to be a pride member."

"I'm sure we can find a way around it if you don't want to be."

"I'm not saying no, but I can't help but wonder how a pride of jaguars will react to having a wolf in their midst."

"Most won't care. Some will, but they're the assholes who shot at us, so I don't care what they think."

"And what about you? You've resisted becoming a pride member for years."

Ford resisted the urge to clear his throat again. "I've been thinking about it. I was keeping my brother at arm's length because I felt like if I allowed him too close, I'd be pulled into the pride, and I wasn't wrong. Spending time with him means spending time with the pride, and it's started to feel like home again."

Ford hadn't expected that. It hadn't been home for most of his life. He'd only lived there until he was eight, and he was almost forty now. Yet, as he started spending more time there, he found that he didn't want to leave. The pride members had been seeing him more often, and they'd softened toward him. The kids he'd played with when he was a child were becoming friends, and the older members remembered him fondly. It was nowhere near as bad as Ford had expected it to be, and he could see himself becoming part of the pride, especially if Madison was with him.

"As long as it's what you want," Madison whispered.

"What I want the most is you. We can figure everything out together if you come home with me."

"It looks like pride territory will be home."

"So it will."

Ford didn't mind. For years, he'd forced himself not to think about what he was missing out on. He couldn't do that anymore, and he didn't want to. He had Madison, and if he stopped being an asshole, he could have the pride and Diego. He'd always have a job with the pride, and when he came home at night, it would be to Madison. He could see them being together for years to come, and while he would have run as far as possible from that in the past, he found that he didn't want to this time. Instead, he wanted to look forward to it and find out what it was like to be in Madison's life and to build a family.

"Let's go home," Madison murmured before kissing Ford again.

As far as Ford was concerned, he already was since he was in Madison's arms.

ABOUT THE AUTHOR

Catherine is the creator of several series, most of them paranormal, including the Whitedell Pride Series and the Gillham Pride Series. While she graduated in translation, she decided to go the writer's way because it was more fun to create her own stories and characters.

She's been living in Italy for more than twenty years, but she's a daughter of the North — Belgium to be precise — and she misses it so much that she's already planning to move back.

She loves pizza — probably too much — her son, her pets, and of course, books. She sneaks some reading time into her schedule every time she has five minutes free from writing, demands from her various pets and son, and lastly, housework.

Connect with her:

lievens.catherine@gmail.com
BookBub: https://www.bookbub.com/authors/catherine-lievens
Website: https://authorcatherinelievens.com/
Facebook: https://www.facebook.com/catherine.lievens.9
Facebook Group: https://www.facebook.com/groups/411788002341528/
Twitter: https://twitter.com/authorCLievens
Newsletter: http://eepurl.com/c-uvKn

www.ingramcontent.com/pod-product-compliance
Lightning Source LLC
Chambersburg PA
CBHW060821120626
46557CB00001B/309